ALSO BY GILES TIPPETTE...

Unforgettable novels of the Old West...

THE BANK ROBBER... When a man's land is stolen out from under him, he has to make a life any way he can...

CHEROKEE... Nothing can stop an honest man from settling a score...

DEAD MAN'S POKER... Outlaw life is a deadly game. But going straight is the biggest gamble of all.

GUNPOINT... There are two things more important than money: honor and survival...

SIXKILLER... No one fights harder than the man who fights for his kin.

HARD ROCK... Rough country breeds a rougher breed of man...

JAILBREAK... When a man's got his back against the wall, there's only one thing to do. Break it down.

AVAILABLE FROM JOVE BOOKS

D0830595

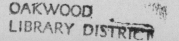

Books by Giles Tippette

Fiction

THE BANK ROBBER
THE TROJAN COW
THE SURVIVALIST
THE SUNSHINE KILLERS
AUSTIN DAVIS
WILSON'S WOMAN
WILSON YOUNG ON THE RUN
THE TEXAS BANK ROBBING COMPANY
WILSON'S GOLD
WILSON'S REVENGE
WILSON'S CHOICE
WILSON'S LUCK
HARD LUCK MONEY
CHINA BLUE
BAD NEWS
CROSS FIRE
JAILBREAK
HARD ROCK
SIXKILLER
GUNPOINT
DEAD MAN'S POKER
CHEROKEE

Nonfiction

THE BRAVE MEN
SATURDAY'S CHILDREN
DONKEY BASEBALL AND OTHER SPORTING DELIGHTS
I'LL TRY ANYTHING ONCE

WILSON'S GOLD

GILES TIPPETTE

JOVE BOOKS, NEW YORK

This Jove Book contains the complete
text of the original edition.
It has been completely reset in a typeface
designed for easy reading and was printed
from new film.

WILSON'S GOLD

A Jove Book / published by arrangement with
the author

PRINTING HISTORY
Jove edition / February 1994

ISBN: 0-515-11311-5

A JOVE BOOK®
Jove Books are published by The Berkley Publishing Group,
200 Madison Avenue, New York, New York 10016.
JOVE and the "J" design are trademarks
belonging to Jove Publications, Inc.

PRINTED IN THE UNITED STATES OF AMERICA

10 9 8 7 6 5 4 3 2 1

To Beverly

CHAPTER 1

"Hell, I heard they'd killed you."

It was a man just down the bar from me. I glanced at him. He was a tall, lanky cowboy in a big hat with his gun set up properly on his hip. He was leaning over his drink, looking down at me. I turned my head back around and went back to my drink.

"I said I thought I'd heard they killed you."

I looked around at him again. "You talking to me?"

"You're Wilson Young, ain't you?"

I looked at him a long moment. He didn't look like law, but then he didn't have to be, as hot as I was. All he had to do was talk too loud and law would shortly arrive.

I was in a saloon in Austin, Texas, way off my range, but the border was a little uncomfortable for me right then.

I glanced around the saloon to see if anyone was listening. Fortunately, the place was almost empty. The bartender was down at the other end, leaning against the wall and dozing.

1

I said: "No, you've got the wrong man."

He squinted his eyes at me and frowned slightly. He had a long, skinny face with a wide mouth. There was a blond stubble on his jaws. After a second he brought his drink and moved down the bar to my side. "I don't think so," he said, saying it low so that it wouldn't get away from just the two of us.

"Yeah," I said. "You have." I was drinking a double whiskey with a glass of beer on the side, and I tried to throw the drink down, intending to leave. The man was making me plenty nervous. There's enough "Wanted" paper out on me in Texas to cover a good-sized hill.

"I'm Chauncey Jones," he said. He put out a hand with a questioning look on his face, as if he were waiting to see what effect his name would have on me. I'd never heard of him. I just glanced down at his hand and back up at his face.

"You don't know me?" He sounded disappointed.

"No," I said, trying to finish my drink.

"I met you in Brownsville three or four years back. You was with them two Richter boys, the cousins I heard got killed on a job with you."

I studied his face, shifting my hip out as I did so that my gun would be free. I didn't like the loose way he was mentioning Les and Tod Richter. In fact, I don't like anybody to mention it. "Listen," I said, saying it slow so he wouldn't misunderstand, "I'm not Wilson

Young, and even if I was I wouldn't tell no loudmouth in a bar. You got that?"

He got a shocked look on his face, and I could see then how young he was. I made him to be no more than twenty-five, five years younger than me in age and about a century in experience. He said: "Oh, hell, I never thought—" He commenced to look embarrassed. "Look, I didn't mean nothing." He glanced around the bar. "Couldn't nobody hear me."

"I'm glad you think that." I drank my beer.

"Look," he said lowly, "I'm in the same business you are. Well, not exactly. But I'm on the dodge myself."

"That don't mean nothing to me."

"I just thought," he said, still fumbling around. "You being here, in Austin. I figured maybe you'd got your troubles fixed up or was fixin' to get them settled an' I—"

"It doesn't matter," I said. "I'm not Wilson Young."

"Oh hell." But he was keeping his voice down. "You're too well-known for that. That's what made me think. You bein' out in the open here in Austin like this. I thought it was all fixed."

I looked at him. He was right about me being well known and about being out in the open in Austin. And if I hadn't of been desperate I'd never have taken such a foolish chance. I'd been hiding out in Mexico for way over a year, and I'd finally got to the place where I was just flat broke. So I'd come to Austin on a fairly harebrained mission to try and get a pretty good slug of money out of a couple of gentlemen I was acquainted with. I'd been careful coming up; riding the back country, staying out of towns, and then seeing the two men on the sly. But when my plans hadn't worked out, I'd been so dumb as to come walkin' into a saloon, albeit a not too busy a-looking saloon, to have a couple of drinks before I started back.

And then I'd run into this loudmouthed buck that recognized me. How was that for luck. For a moment I didn't quite know what to do. Run quick and take the chance of having law after me, or stay and try and convince him I wasn't who he thought I was.

He said: "But I still heard they killed you. Down on the border. What the hell happened?"

I looked away, remembering the gunfight in the hotel in Nuevo Laredo, staggering toward the railroad tracks and falling down in a ditch. Then coming to in an adobe house three days later. I didn't like to think about it. It seemed years ago.

"What have I got to do," I asked him, keeping my voice reasonable, "to convince you I ain't Wilson Young?" I added, "Whoever the hell that is."

"But you are," he said earnestly.

I said, still keeping my voice reasonable, "Then, if I was, do you think it's very smart of you to keep pressing it like this? If I was Wilson Young, don't you think you'd be taking a hell of a chance of getting some light let through your middle?"

"I know that," he said, still earnestly. "But I got to take the chance. I got some business I want to talk over with you. You come in a while ago, and I thought it was the damnedest stroke of luck I'd ever run up on. I been standin' down there for ten minutes, tryin' to think of some way to up and speak to you."

"So you choose that I-heard-you-was-killed in business."

"That's about the size of it."

I laughed. "Sorry to disappoint you." I pitched some coins on the bar, set my hat straight, and walked by him out the door.

But he wouldn't have that. He followed me out to my horse. "Look here," he said, "look, just let me talk to you a minute. Honest to God, I got a little piece of business I know you'd be interested in."

I got up on my horse and glanced around. We were on a little side street that was deserted. It was coming June and was hot. I gathered the reins in my hand. "Listen to me," I said, "I'm not interested in any business. You got that?" The more I looked at him the more he sounded and acted like Tod Richter. And Tod, without Les thrown in to balance the scales, was never no prize.

"Listen," he said, taking hold of a tie string on my saddle, "we could make a hell of a ton of money. And it's just a two-man job. Honest, it's as sure as mother's milk."

I was about to rein away when I seen a man walking toward us. He was still a good way off, but the way that sun hit that town marshal's badge on his chest, and the casual way he was carrying that shotgun, left no doubt in my mind that it was law. And here the fool was grabbing on to my saddle and making a commotion. The law hadn't looked our way yet, but I figured if I rode off, the damn fool would probably chase me on foot, yelling no doubt, and *that* would get some attention.

I said, low and hard: "Where can we talk?" It seemed the easiest way to get shut of him.

"I got a room at the Driskell Hotel," he said.

"The Driskell! Hell, that's right in the middle of town!" It was also a damn first-class hotel, and it made me wonder what a buck like Chauncey would be doing in such a place.

"We can come around up the back on it," he said. "I'll get my horse." Before I could say another word he'd stepped down to the next hitch post and untied a good-looking roan gelding that was out of good stock or I wasn't no judge of horseflesh.

Not knowing what else to do I reined my horse out in the street so as to sort of hide my face from the town law as he passed. Still, I was nervous and sweating, and Chauncey Jones was taking forever to get his goddamn horse untied. "Hurry up!" I said in a low, harsh voice.

Then he was mounted and we rode off just before the marshal came up to us.

I rode down the street, following the young buck, cursing bitterly under my breath at the idiotic fix I'd managed to get myself in. I could, of course, turn and ride off, but he might just as likely spur after me, calling attention to both of us, and that was the last thing I wanted. No, I decided, the best thing to do would be to get him alone in his hotel room—if we made it that far—and then give him a little lesson in manners and quietly make my way out of town.

We sort of circled around the town, taking back streets whenever we could. I kept my hat kind of pulled low, but not so low that I couldn't see everything that was happening. I didn't trust the man that was leading me. Why should I? I hadn't known him ten minutes, and in my past line of work you get to where you don't trust much of nobody. I had already resolved in my mind that if anything funny happened he was going to be the first to go down. I cantered up almost abreast of him and gave him that information.

He said, "My God, Mr. Young, don't worry."

I told him I was going to be a half-stride behind him the rest of the way, and that I hoped, for his sake, that nothing happened.

We came up, finally, behind the Driskell and dismounted and tied up. I didn't loosen the cinch on my horse for I didn't intend to be long. But Chauncey did on his.

We went through the rear door of the hotel, and my, it was a grand place. It had marble columns in the lobby, with rugs on the floor and a bunch of big, overstuffed chairs and divans sitting all over the place. The lobby itself was about as big as two barns, rising up in the air at least fifteen or sixteen feet. They even had a bar over at one end. We come up a little short flight of steps, our spurs jingling against the stone walls, and paused to look the layout over.

"You want a drink?" Chauncey asked, nodding at the bar.

"Don't play the calf," I said. "Let's get up to your goddamn room."

We went up a back stairs, going up three flights, and then down a long hall to his room. It was a pretty plush-looking layout, with a bed and a chair and a wash table. Even had a carpet on the floor. I figured it must have cost him three or four dollars a day, which is considerable when you figure it was just a place to sleep. Man don't make no money when he's asleep.

Chauncey said did I want a drink, and I said get it out. He went under his washstand and come out with a bottle of good bourbon and two glasses and poured for both of us.

"Luck," I said, and held mine up. He repeated the toast and we drank.

I took the chair and he sat down on the bed, sort of half-leaning back on his elbows. "Boy," he said, looking into the half-drink he still had in his glass, "I never figured to get so lucky, Mr. Young."

"Don't call me Mr. Young."

"Well, all right, Wilson."

"And don't call me that neither." I turned my glass up and finished what I had, grateful for it. I meant, before I put the skids on the boy, to get me the amount of drink I'd meant to get when I'd gone in that saloon in the first place and he'd so rudely interrupted me.

He looked confused. "Well, what should I call you? Do I call you Will?"

"No, not that either," I said.

"Look here, you are Wilson Young." He raised up full on the bed. "I know that for a goddamn fact!"

"Gettin' mouthy again, ain't you?"

"All right," he said. "I done wrong comin' at you like I did, but I got excited and never give it no thought. All I was thinkin' was here you'd come along, just when I was wonderin' who in the world I could get to go in with me on this job, and I guess I didn't play it too smart."

"You shore didn't," I agreed.

"Well, what the goddamn hell!" he said, just a touch of belligerence in his voice.

I looked at him. "If you can get that goddamn excited over what you think is a little piece of luck, just how nervous will you get in a real sweat? Give me some more of that bourbon."

He got up and poured me out a pretty good slug. I drank half of it off, looking at him over the top of the glass, appraising him. My one thought was how to get away from this fool without his raising a ruckus. I figured I might catch him unawares and give him a solid tap with my pistol barrel and put him out for a while. I didn't want to punch him with my fist for that can hurt your hands and don't generally knock nobody out with one lick, not anybody as big as this kid was. Of course the logical thing to do would be to hear his proposition out, thank him kindly for the drink and the offer, and then ride on out as I had been intending to. But, and I swear it, I wasn't sure I could get away from this big galoot that easy. What he said subsequently didn't do anything to reassure me.

He said: "You don't know what an honor this is for me, Mr. Young."

I grimaced. "Will you cut that shit out. I told you not to call me Mr. Young."

"Yessir, I know. But it just comes natural because I admire you so much, sir."

And he meant it. I sat there looking at his bright young face and wished he knew what my past several years had been like. I didn't expect he'd be doing so much admiring then.

I got my name less by being a successful bank robber than by being a killer of men. In what little defense I can muster for such a sorry appellation let me say that I don't recollect ever setting out to kill anybody deliberately. It had always seemed like circumstances had contrived to put me in the situation where I'd had to draw my gun against another man, and the inevitable result had been that it was the other man that had always gotten killed.

I had come from a good family. My folks were landed quality in south Texas, my dad owning a considerable spread until the carpetbaggers and scalawag politicians had robbed him of it right after the Civil War. But in spite of that I'd still gotten a better education than most, going on up through ten years of public schooling, which was about the time everything went to hell and I'd lit out on my own.

I am not playing the calf when I say I never meant to drift into outlawry, but I guess a man will do damn near anything if he gets hungry enough, and that's about the way it went with me.

I engaged in shiftless and petty robberies until I fell in to the road agent business and from there, after I'd joined up with the Richter boys, whom I'd grown up with around Corpus Christi, had gradually drifted into the profession of bank robbing.

We never made no good thing out of it. In fact, what brought me to my lowly estate, sitting in a hotel room busted and broke down at the heels and listening to a damn fool young buck, had been the bank-robbing business, especially the last two jobs we'd tried to pull. On the first of the two, at Carrizo Springs, Tod had lost a damn good horse and the four thousand in gold we'd taken out of the bank when we'd tried to cross the Rio Grande at flood stage. The next, at Uvalde, had been Howland Thomas's proposition. About the only good thing that came out of that was Howland had got his worthless ass killed. Unfortunately, his partner, Chico, had also got killed as well as Tod. And Les—

Well, I have to say that Les also got killed as a result of that attempted robbery, for that was what had caused them two Cattlemen's Protective detectives to cross the border in pursuit of us and kill Les in Nuevo Laredo.

Of course I later killed both of them, arriving too late from Sabinas Hidalgo where I'd been pursuing the Mexican girl, but I'd killed them while Les was laying up in the infirmary dying, killing the last one, Bob Bird, even as he was dead.

And taking three bullets from Bird myself. One in the side, one in the right shoulder, and one under the collarbone. Then collapsing in that ditch by the side of the railroad tracks and coming to in that adobe house.

I don't know how I lived. It was two old ladies and a teenaged boy, Mexicans, that had drug me in. Why they did it and why they hid me and nursed me is a riddle for the sages to answer. You've got to remember that Nuevo Laredo is one of the roughest border towns there is. And why they'd take a shot-up gringo in and waste their food and care and medicines on him is more than I can think.

I know I come to about four days later, best I could figure, after I'd been shot. Come to and one of them old ladies run for a pot of beef gruel. I'm gonna tell you, they set great store by that beef broth. They crammed that down me until I believe I willed myself to have strength enough to get away from that outstretched wooden spoon.

I guess I was there about six weeks. They nursed me with herbs and poultices and all them other old-wives' remedies. Which, as bad as I was shot up, was about like trying to cure a broken leg with linament. I figure I pulled through because I was meant to more than anything they done.

Not that I wasn't all-out grateful. I was. They saved my life when they pulled me out of that ditch and drug me inside and got some food down me to get my strength up. They fussed over me and fidgeted and sat up with me and prayed over me and lit candles and done all that. And they hid me out from the law. I truly believe that they wrought what was to be considered a miracle, given the circumstances and all that.

So I felt gratitude and love in my heart for them ladies and that young boy. And when I left I left them what money I could and promised to come back. They patted my cheek and wished me well, and I haven't seen them since.

Though I intend to again.

I left going back to where I'd come from. Going back to try and see that girl again, fleeing into the interior of Mexico true enough, but fleeing back to where I hoped I could make some contact with Linda again.

It's a little hard to explain about the girl, especially when you understand I'd only seen her twice. And both of them times had been under strict supervisions so that we'd only ever exchanged just the barest few words. I guess, if I were honest, I'd admit that she'd come to represent some kind of dream to me. Maybe the dream of the kind of man I'd meant to be in the first place. A good man, an honest man, a man of quality that could go his own way without having to sneak hither and yon, a man that could hold his head up amongst his neighbors without having to feel ashamed for the sorry estate he'd come down to.

I guess she represented quality to me.

I first met her at her uncle's ranchero outside of Villa Guerro whence we'd gone to try and trade for a horse to replace the one that Tod had lost in the river. I can still remember the way she looked when she come sweeping into that room. About nineteen or twenty years old with raven hair, wearing a white *mantilla*, her bosoms straining at the bodice of her lace-lined velvet dress, her hips swelling away from that tiny waist.

Not that it was with the eyes of lust that I viewed her. There was that, too, of course, for after all, a man is still a man. No, it was much more than that, it was like seeing the very living image of your dreams come walking in to you. We did nothing more than exchange bows and curtseys before her uncle sent her off. But she'd stopped, just as she was leaving the room, and sent me the longest, most searching look, a look that pierced its way straight into my heart.

It's difficult to understand how strongly that moment with Linda had affected me. It made me see myself, made me ashamed of myself, made me aspire to do more. We'd come there to her uncle's place, who was a true don and *grandee*, with a mouthful of lies about being cattle buyers and so on. The truth was we was broke, unsuccessful bank robbers. And that old don had still treated us with that rare courtesy that only men of quality and estate seem to have.

Well, I'd vowed to change. I wanted to be worthy of that girl. I wanted to be able to court her and bid for her hand like a man of quality also. She had affected me so much that I told Les, when we were on our way to pull that robbery with Howland and Chico at that bank in Uvalde, that it was my last job.

"I'll get me a stake out of this," I'd said, "and when I'm through I'm going down into Mexico and set up for a horse breeder."

He'd said: "You can't do it, Will. You are what you are and you can't change."

But I'd made a start on it. After that disastrous robbery, when it was just me and Les left, we'd split up—him going to Nuevo Laredo and me taking it on down to Sabinas Hidalgo, where her father's ranch was, to try and meet Linda and to try and get in a position where I could court her.

I'd still come in with a mouthful of lies, representing myself as a horse breeder who intended to set up right there in Sabinas. But it hadn't all been lies. Part of it, the intentions part, had been true. The only thing I'd lacked was the money. I'd got invited in by her daddy, asked to supper, and had the almost unbearable thrill of having her touch my hand and call my name, even if it was just for a brief, fleeting second.

But that second had told me she was feeling somewhat the same way I was, and that was enough encouragement for me.

And then had come that telegram from a mutual friend about Les laying near to dying in that infirmary in Nuevo Laredo.

So I'd gone. And the rest had just happened.

After that I'd gone back into the interior, but I hadn't gone near Sabinas Hidalgo. I was broker than ever, and I knew I had to get me a stake if I was gonna have a chance at that young filly's hand. So I didn't even propose to show my face until I could come in with honor and a chance to do what I'd said I was going to do.

I'd done one thing; I stayed straight. Of course I'd never have committed no depredations in Mexico, anyway. A man don't foul his own nest, and, right then, Mexico was the only safe place for me.

But I couldn't make any money. The kind of work I could do was the kind a hundred peons could do and would do for a fourth of the money. Hell, I fell to some low estates in them days. Once I was even a bank guard on some money that was being transferred from one bank to another.

That was a laugh.

But I sure couldn't make any money. Not only couldn't make enough to give thought to saving up a stake, I wouldn't even make enough to live on.

That's when I'd got so desperate I'd decided to come into Austin and look up the two gentlemen I thought mighty could benefit me some. I'd pinned some high hopes on it, too, some might high hopes.

But them high hopes, like most high hopes, had ridden in and taken their duly prophesied fall.

So there it was. I was desperate for money. I was desperate to win the hand of that girl and salvage what little was left of my life. I was willing to do almost anything. My mission, my hopeless mission, to Austin had proven that.

So this was me, this was the Wilson Young that the foolish buck of a boy insisted on calling sir and mister. This was the famous outlaw that was sitting across from him in a high-class hotel room drinking his quality bourbon. A bourbon and a room that I couldn't have afforded myself. If the truth be known, I had two dollars and a little change on my person. That and a pretty second-rate horse. I guess that bit as deep as anything, because I'd never rode anything but high-class blooded stock. A man in the line of work I'd been in always wants to be well mounted because he never knows when he's going to have to depend on the animal between his legs to haul his ass out of the trouble he's found.

One of the best horses I'd ever owned had been a little filly that I'd been riding when we pulled that last job. She'd been where I'd left her in Mexico after I'd recovered from my wounds, but I'd ended up having to sell her. A man as poor as I'd become can't afford no high-priced blooded horse.

It had hurt me to sell her, hurt me more than just losing the filly. It had hurt me to know that I'd come down so far I couldn't even afford a good horse.

And that's low. For a man like myself.

Now I took a sip of my drink and looked across at Chauncey Jones, as he called himself.

"Tell me about yourself, *hombre*," I said. I was looking at him steadily, looking to see what degree of nervousness that would produce in him.

But he was relaxed. He just shrugged, leaned back on the bed, and said: "Ain't one hell of a lot to tell."

I raised my eyebrows slightly. "Must be. Here you are a pretty young man, and here you're living in a damn fancy hotel, drinking damn fancy whiskey, and riding a damn good horse." I squinted. "And them look to be damn good yard goods you're wearing there. You didn't get all that just by singin' loud in church. Yore daddy buy them for you?"

"Hell, Wilson, don't say things like that to me." His face got bitter, and he didn't look so young. "My daddy never bought me shit.

Ever'thing I got I got on my own."

"Yeah? How?"

"I told you I was on the dodge. Told you I'd been on the scout. I robbed for it, what do you think?"

"What'd you do, find a little old lady carrying a chunk of money down a dark alley?"

His face flushed. I wasn't consciously trying to make him angry, it just kept coming out.

"Now listen," he said, with a little heat in his voice, "you ain't got no call to talk to me like that, even if you are Wilson Young. I know I ain't in your caliber, but I never claimed to be. But what I got I got by my own hand, and it wasn't robbin' no old ladies, nor no children neither!"

I laughed. Then I motioned for him to pour me another drink. He'd cost me enough trouble. The least he could do was furnish the liquor.

I said: "Well, tell me about these outlaw days of yours. Where'd you make your score? Robbing banks?"

"Naw," he said, flushing a little and looking down. "You know better than that."

"Well, what then?" I asked him, prompting.

"Aaaww." He looked away. "You might think less of me if I was to tell you the truth."

"I'd think less," I said, "if you don't."

"Well . . ." Still he hesitated. "Well, it ain't much of a story for a man to tell."

"Give me another drink," I said. I sipped, looking at him, waiting for him to go on. "Tell me this evil deed you've done."

"Well," he said. He looked away and then said, almost inaudibly, "I was—I was always kind of hell with the ladies."

"Good for you," I said dryly, feeling my own womanlessness.

"I ain't bragging about it, you know," he said, defense in his tone.

"Get on with it. Tell me what you've got to tell. Hell, I've got a long ride to make and no time to sit here listening to hemming and hawing. Tell me about your bandit days."

"That makes it harder," he said.

"What's that got to do with it?" I was growing impatient. It was time to be on the road. Every moment I sat in Austin only added to my danger.

"Well," he finally said, hesitantly, "what happened was I married this girl who was the daughter of a prosperous rancher down in south Texas."

"That's a crime?" I looked at him curiously.

"The way it worked out it was. See," he said, "see, what happened, was that her daddy was so grateful for me takin' her off his hands. I mean marrying her 'cause her prospects was none too good." He blushed a little. "What I mean to say was that she wasn't no beauty. I mean her daddy was some sort of grateful. And he'd kind of taken such a liking to me that it wasn't long before he was kind of letting me handle some of the affairs of the ranch." He paused. "Such as the books and so on. Handlin' some of the buying and selling. You understand?"

"I'm starting to," I said.

"Well, anyway, it come down to a place where there was a considerable amount of cash on hand and I— Well, I taken it and lit out. They's a word for what I done. I don't recollect it right off."

"It's called stealing," I said.

"That's not what they call it on the posters. Anyway—" he said, letting it hang.

"How much did you get?"

"Right at six thousand dollars."

I whistled lowly. "How long ago was that?"

"Little over a year. They only put wanted notices out on me some six months back. I think the girl kept hoping I'd come back and talked her daddy into laying off me."

I studied him for a long moment. "You're something," I finally said. "Really something."

"Well, hell!" he said, his hackles coming up a little. "I done what I could with what I had."

The phrase hit home. It startled me. I'd once told an old aunt, who'd accused me of going bad, almost the very same thing. Looking at the boy, boy in spite of his age, I could see, now that I was looking at him without the fear of the law suddenly taking me, that he was good-looking in a way that would appeal to women. He felt my gaze and smiled shame-facedly.

"Give me another drink," I said.

He poured it out and then leaned forward earnestly. "Look here," he said, "let me tell you

what I wanted to talk to you about. This job I
got in mind."

"Okay," I said. "It's your whiskey."

"Well, what it is," he said, looking straight
at me, "is that I want we should rob a train."

CHAPTER 2

I just looked at him for a long moment, recollecting what he'd said about a two-man job. Finally, I said: "You want to do what?"

"I want we should go and rob a train." He said it earnestly, looking as if he were talking about a ride around the block.

"I see," I said. I held my glass out. "If you'll give me one more drink of that I'll take it for a stirrup cup and be on my way."

He looked startled. "Don't you want to hear about it?"

"No," I said. "I'm going to get the hell out of here before I catch whatever's wrong with you."

"But look here!" he said. "You've—"

"Look, cowboy. Robbin' trains ain't a good occupation at the best. Thinkin' you can rob a train as a two-man job is about like standing outside at night and lettin' the moon shine in your mouth instead of eating supper. No, you're loco. So I'll just finish this and be on my way."

He stood up, looking a little wild-eyed. "Now wait a minute! Look here, you can't just up and walk out of here like this."

"I can't?" I asked, amused.

"No sir! Look here, I've done told you about this job I've got planned. You can't just walk out on that kind of information."

"Son, believe me, your secret is safe with me. I can promise you I won't talk to nobody about no two-man train-robbing jobs. It's bad enough they want me for jail, I don't want to run the risk of gettin' put in the loony bin as well."

"But listen to me!" he insisted. "It ain't as crazy as you may think. Just give me a chance to explain it."

"I don't think so," I said. I yawned. My drink was almost gone, and I was about ready to hit the trail. Though God knows what I thought I'd do or where I'd go or how long I'd last with two dollars in my pocket.

"It ain't crazy," he said again. "And it don't mean holding up a whole train. It's got to do with them transporting gold money down to the border. It's just one car. Please, Mr. Young, listen to me."

Something in his voice caught me. It had a little of that little-boy-in-wonder quality. Or perhaps it was the mention of gold coin. I don't know. But I frowned at him. "All right," I said, "I got about five more minutes. And it's your whiskey. So talk away."

Well, I heard him out and he was right. It was a two-man job. It was risky, but it could be done. And if it got done, and done right, there was a hell of a payoff.

That is if what he was saying was straight.

I sat and looked at him for a long time after he'd finished. I didn't want to say anything, didn't want to sound interested, didn't even want to get myself interested. I sat there thinking about it, turning it over in my mind. He'd said that the locals down along the border, where there was a great deal of trade between Mexico and Texas, didn't like dealing in greenbacks, that they didn't trust that paper money. That the majority of the money in use was gold coin. Well, that part was straight enough. I knew that myself. Then he'd said that on the last day of every month there was a special car added to the train that ran from San Antonio to Laredo and that that car contained anywhere from forty thousand dollars to fifty thousand dollars in gold coin, money sent down from a federal bank in San Antonio to the banks in Laredo.

"Then," he'd said, "they bring the paper dollars back on up here to San Antonio. But the place to take it is on the trip down. Even though the gold weighs more than the greenbacks."

"Why's that?" I'd asked him.

"See this car has got an air hole in the top that's got a cover on it. It's locked, but I've got me a key. Anyways, just about a mile after she pulls out of the station and is just about outside, the train passes by this tool shack right by the tracks. Just a little old short drop down on to the train and it ain't goin' fast at all. Then—" He'd slapped his hands together, "unlock that cover, drop down in amongst one surprised clerk, and you got the gold."

"Only thing," I'd noted, with just a touch of sarcasm, "is that you're on the inside with the gold on a moving train. What then?"

"Best part," he'd said, grinning like a schoolboy. "Train takes on water about seventy-five, eighty miles down the track. Just a little one-man joint. I'm already there with the horses. You unlock the car from the inside, we unload it, and wham bam, thank you ma'am—we're gone. With forty thousand dollars."

Now I got out a little black Mexican *cigarrillo* and lit it, still looking at him. "How do you know this?" I finally asked him.

"I just know," he said vaguely.

"Bullshit on that," I said. "Exactly how?"

He looked uncomfortable. Finally he said: "It was my daddy-in-law, the one I stole the money off of. He was one of the ones got the banks to go to doing it. Him and some of them other big ranchers down there near the border."

"And the key? Where'd you get that?"

"That wasn't so easy," he admitted. "See, after I taken the money and cut and run I went up to old San Antone, kinda hangin' around and hidin' out. But I kept thinkin' about that bank car so I commenced lurkin' around the railway yards. Finally I spotted it. I taken a good long time studyin' it, week maybe and just at night. Finally I seen that air vent on top, and I clumbed up there and seen it was locked with a plain old padlock. I memorized the kind and the name and hunted around town 'til I found one just like it, then, one black night, I clumb back up there and hacksawed off the old one and put on the one I had a key for. That was a week ago."

I stared at him, a little impressed by his ingenuity. "Hmmmm," I said, drawing on my cigarette. "What's below the lid on that air vent? A screen?"

"Nothin'," he said. "I think they just use it in the winter when they got a potbellied stove goin' inside. I raised the cover and I could see that stove down there. Thing is, I don't reckon too many people know about them haulin' that gold coin."

"I don't know," I said doubtfully. I frowned. "What are you doing in Austin, anyway, when the job's in San Antonio?"

"Lookin' for you," he said frankly. "Or somebody like you. Some high-class professional that kin help me pull this off."

"I don't know," I said. "The whole thing sounds damn risky to me. What if there's more than one guard in the car?"

"Aw, hell. They won't be. And even if they was you could handle them, Mr. Young."

"Me? Who the hell said it was going to be me going in the car? How about you going in the car and I tend to the business at the watering station."

"Now that ain't common sense, Mr. Young,"
he said earnestly. "You know and I know that
you're a lot more able to take care of armed
guards in a bank car than I am. That's plain
and no disputing it."

"Shit," I said. I leaned back in the chair,
thinking on it. But God I felt so low and so
broke and so dispirited I felt like going home
with the armadillo and getting down in his
burrow and pulling the top in after me. It ain't
a good feeling to not have a home and only two
dollars and a sorry horse between you and star-
vation, let alone between you and your dreams.

Chauncey looked at me expectantly, watching me smoke and think. He poured my glass
full while I let my mind play with the situation.

Hell, I thought, I've quit this game. I've give
it up. I'm through. That's what I told Les.

But just one more stake.

Just one stake where I could set up the
horse-breeding business in Mexico and court
that high-class, lovely girl.

Just one stake.

Oh God, it hurt so bad to just have two dollars in your pocket and be unable to walk up
to a door and be considered quality.

But this was a harebrained scheme.

That might work, could work if I could just
but bring it off.

I sat smoking, these thoughts running
through my head. Thinking of the girl Linda.
Thinking of that fine family in Sabinas Hidalgo,

that fine ranchero. Thinking of the way they'd received me and believed that I was the man I claimed to be. How grand it would be to actually be that man.

And I could be with the stake I could get off a job such as this.

Chauncey was still watching me. I said, "I don't know. Let me think about this."

"Com'on, Will," he urged. "It'd be so easy."

"Shut up, fool!" I said brutally. "You wouldn't know easy from buttermilk. So shut up!"

"Will," he said, sort of begging, "look here, I want me a gun-robbing job. Can you understand that? I'm about half-ashamed of the way I robbed my wife's daddy and I'd like to do it right. Do it like you done it."

I stared at him. "Why, you goddamn fool!" I said. "You're a bigger goddamn fool than I thought you were. You want to go off like some little boy with a play pistol and point it at folks. Are you crazy? Shit, that kind of talk I wouldn't rob a piggy bank with you."

"Aw, Will," he said.

I got up, walked to the window, and looked out. The street was busy, horsemen and buggies and people afoot hurrying back and forth. I looked down, wondering what the hell I was doing. But then what were my prospects anyway?

I looked around at Chauncey. "What's the day of the month?"

"Fourteenth, I think," he said. He thought a second. "Yeah, it's the fourteenth."

"And this train goes on the last day of the month?"

"That's when she goes."

I turned and crossed the room and sat back down in my chair. I took off my hat and put it on my knee. "Well, lad," I said, "we got a problem."

His face clouded.

I said: "Even if I was willing to do this job, I can't."

"Why not? Listen, I'm really counting on this."

"A simple reason," I said. "I hate to disillusion you, Chauncey, but the great Wilson Young is flat broke. Busted on his ass. I've got two dollars to my name, and that ain't money enough for me to hang around this part of the country without being detected. So I've got to get on back down to Mexico and try and scratch me out a living."

His face cleared. "Is that all? Hell, I'll stake you, Will. My God, I thought it was something serious." He got out his wallet and began leafing out bills. "Couple of hundred do you?"

I looked at him steadily. Not really surprised. "You want to do this job that bad?"

"Hell, yes," he said. "It's a ton of money and ought to be easy as pie."

I kept on looking at him. He was holding the money out. "I've got to have a good horse," I said. "That nag I'm riding ain't worth a damn, and if I'm going on any cross-country getaways

I want some decent horseflesh between my legs."

"That's easy," he said. "Why don't you take three hundred." He got the extra money out of his wallet and held it out toward me.

I looked at it a long moment. Hell, I believe I could have asked him for a thousand, and he'd of come up with it. "All right," I finally said. I took the money, folded it, and put it in my shirt pocket. Then I put on my hat. "Now let's go get something to eat. All this drinkin' and talkin' has made me hungry."

He was right behind me as we started out the door. I suddenly whirled and slapped him backhanded across the face. I'd already made up my mind that if he didn't have enough sand to draw I wouldn't do the job with him. But he did. Or he tried to, which was good enough for me. I had my own iron in my hand before his had cleared leather.

He stumbled back a step or two. He stood there staring at my gun, his eyes wide and surprised. "Shit!" he said.

I holstered my gun. "Don't worry," I said. "It was just a little test."

He didn't relax right away. It took him a good second to turn loose of his own revolver and let it slide back in the holster. Finally he said, "Jesus Christ!" He said it low, but with force.

"Sorry," I said. "But they say a scare is good for a man's liver. Cleans him out."

He went, "Whoooosh," and said, "I can do without it."

"Fine. Now we got a deal. Let's go get something to eat. We'll find some out-of-the-way place. We're leaving for San Antonio tomorrow."

CHAPTER 3

It had been a good while since I'd been in San Antonio, and I was surprised to see how the place had grown. We put up at a good hotel, taking a room together, not so much to save money as to give me a chance to scout out my new partner a little better. I ain't never been one for taking on partners as a general rule, and taking one on in the short acquaintance I'd had with Mr. Chauncey Jones was a good indication of how hard up I was.

First day Chauncey was all aflame to drag me down to the railroad yards and show me that money car. But I made him set still. I wanted to look over the whole layout and see just how well known I might be in the town and just how freely I could move around. First night we had a good supper at the hotel and then spent time in a few low-class saloons that I figured would give me a lead on who was in town. There's folks on *both* sides of the law don't wish me any good, and I wanted to find out just who all I might need to be alert for.

We were in about our third joint of the night, a smoky little rotgut mill with the usual bunch of ruffians and drunks hangs around such places in a town the size of San Antonio. Me and Chauncey were sitting at one of the tables drinking cognac. Chauncey had started off pretty heavy, but I'd slowed him down and we're nursing our drinks. The only thing was he insisted on talking, and the more he talked the less he impressed me as someone I wanted to go into the train-robbing business with. Once I'd told him, "For God's sake, Chauncey, shut your damn mouth. You sound like a sixteen-year-old boy playactin' at being grown-up."

It had checked him some, but hadn't brought him to a sliding stop.

Chauncey said: "Hell, Will, let's get down to the railroad yard."

"Take it easy," I answered. "We got plenty of time."

"But I want you to see how easy it's going to be." He was playing with his glass, sliding it back and forth from one hand to another across the wet tabletop.

"Listen, Chauncey," I said. "You are commencing to worry me. We'll go to the railroad yard when I'm good and ready and not before."

That made him sull up, making him remind me of Tod more and more. And that wasn't a compliment.

There were a line of men at the bar, and one of the backs looked familiar. He was a big man wearing a short, brush popper's leather jacket and a big, flat-crowned, flat-brimmed black hat. He had his denims tucked in his boots and he was wearing big rowled Mexican spurs that almost drug on the floor. He was hunched over, looking straight ahead. Every once in a while he'd tip his head back and take a pretty good jolt of whiskey. I knew him, had known him for a long time.

"Set still," I said to Chauncey. "I'll be right back."

"Where you going?" He looked like he was going to rise.

"Just set!" I said. I got up and walked quietly up and stood behind the man. After a second I leaned near his ear and said, "You look like a cattle thief to me. From the front or the back."

He didn't turn around, just slowly straightened and stiffened. He let his hand come loose from his glass and drop down by his right side, near the big pistol.

I said: "You reach for that thing and I'll stick a tamale up your ass, greaser." I was speaking so quietly that the men on either side didn't know anything was happening.

The man turned, slowly, moving his head first and then letting the rest of his body follow.

"Hello, Negro," I said in Spanish. "What the hell you doing out of jail?"

Then he recognized me, and a big grin hit his face, making his teeth very white against his dark skin. We called him Negro because he was so dark. He was what you call a black Mexican, black beyond a Mexican's natural brown. Then he always had a scrubbly black whisker growth on his face that made him look even blacker.

"Eh, *chumacho!*" he said. He gave me a big hug, in the Spanish fashion, pounding me on the back. "What you say, *hombre?*"

"Not a hell of a lot," I admitted. "What are you doing so far off your range? You can't steal no cattle up here?"

"Eh, what you talkin' about? I been in the banking business." He gave me a wink.

"Yeah? Well, com'on over to the table and tell me about it. Or any other lies you got handy."

We walked back over to the table, and I introduced him to Chauncey who was about to bust with curiosity.

I'd known Chulo for a good many years. I never knew what his proper name was. When we didn't call him Negro, we called him Chulo, which is more a nickname than anything else. We'd never done any business together, but we'd always been friendly, and, once, he'd backed me in a saloon fight in Reynosa when I'd got myself in a kind of bind. As far as I was concerned he was a good steady man that I wouldn't be ashamed to partner with. The last I'd heard of him he'd been stealing cattle in Mexico and selling them in the United States.

"Now what's this lie about going in the banking business?"

He laughed while Chauncey poured him out a drink of the cognac. "Oh, I did a little bank business in Mexico," he said grinning hugely. "A very nice little town with a *bonito* little bank."

I snorted. "You better leave them damn Mexican banks alone," I said. "They'll hang you. Or worse. Make much of a load?"

He pulled a face. "There were too many of us. It was the *hombres* I did the cattle business with. And there were so many that no man got much." Then he grinned again. "But we shot the hell out of that bank, for sure."

"So now you're hidin' out here in the States, eh? Way up from the border."

"*¿Cómo no?*" he said. "I thin' I give them some time to forget. Mexicans have short memories. Pretty soon I go back."

"Well, I'm glad to see you, Chulo," I said. I clicked glasses with him and knocked back a toast to luck.

"*Buena suerte*," he said. "Always."

Chauncey was looking back and forth as we talked, dying to get a word in. I didn't want him saying anything about the job to Chulo, not because I didn't trust the Negro, but just because it ain't good business to do much talking about a job.

"And you, *mi amigo*?" Chul asked me. "You are off your range also. Business?"

"Yeah," I said, giving Chauncey a look. "But it ain't set so I don't want to talk about it."

Chulo said, "Ah," but Chauncey, about to bust, put in, "What do you mean, Will, it ain't set? I thought we had a deal."

I looked at him sourly. "Chauncey, shut your goddamn mouth. And if I have to remind you again to quit calling me by name I'm gonna kick your ass up between your shoulder blades."

Chauncey looked hurt and Chulo was amused. The Negro looked over at the young man and said, "You must not be afraid of this *caballero*. If he chooses to kill you it is done so quick as to be almost painless. Can one ask for better?"

"Listen," I said, "save your goddamn greaser advice for somebody that ain't quite so skittish. This one is still a little young."

"He's big enough," Chulo said, looking Chauncey over like he was a head of beef.

"About half-mouth," I said.

"Aw, Will," Chauncey said, looking down at the table, embarrassed. I was deliberately being rough on him. It was best to get him shut of his scatterbrained habits before the play got serious.

About that time a drunk stumbled in to Chulo and spilled a drink down his front. "¡*Mierda*!" the Negro swore and shoved the man away so hard that he stumbled and fell. "Look at this!" Chulo said, brushing the whiskey off his shirt. "What a mess!"

I was watching Chulo and not paying any attention to the drunk he'd shoved until I heard a shout and swerved my head to the left. The drunk was up and had drawn a pistol and was leveling down on the Negro. "Chulo!" I yelled, but it was Chauncey that

made the play. Before I could react he had
swung out of his chair, knocked the drunk's
gun hand up and, in the same motion, hit him
a stunning right-hand. The drunk dropped like
a wagon had fell on him. Then, without pausing,
Chauncey dropped on the man's chest, hit him
a hard right and left, then jumped up, grabbed
the drunk by the shirt, and dragged him out
the door and threw him in the street. He came
back, breathing a little hard, but looking satis-
fied with himself.

I stared at him then glanced across at Chulo.

The Negro said, raising his heavy eyebrows,
"This is a very quick young man."

"Surprised the hell out of me," I admitted. I
looked at Chauncey. "That was all right."

"I thank you," was all Chulo said.

"Aw, he was just a drunk," Chauncey said.
"Wadn't nothin' to it." But the attempt at mod-
esty was hard pressed to hide how pleased he
was with himself. "Just an old drunk," he said
again. "Couldn't harm a flea."

Chulo said, "No, let me disagree. There you
are mistaken. He is the most dangerous kind."
He looked over at me.

What he said was true. For people in our line
of work it's that drunk or that incompetent idiot that will kill you because you don't take them
seriously enough and don't pay them the close
attention you would in dealing with somebody
that's really capable. And that's when you get
shot in the back, or surprised like Chulo had
almost been. You can't predict them, can't know

what they're going to do. You'll turn your back on ninety-nine of them, and the hundredth will blow your head off. It's one of the hazards of living on the hair-trigger all the time. You let down at the wrong time and and you're dead.

"Old drunk like that?" Chauncey said, looking at Chulo. "Shoot!"

The black Mexican smiled slightly. "You will learn. If you have time."

"Hell with it," Chauncey said. "Let's have a drink."

The bar had gone back to business as usual and we sat quietly, drinking and talking for another half-hour. Finally I got up. "Well, Chulo, gettin' late. We got to haul our freight." I told him the hotel we were staying in and the room number. He was staying with a cousin. "Drag on by tomorrow," I told him. "And we'll get in a little daylight drinking."

"How long you be in town?"

I shrugged. "*¿Quién sabe?* Who knows?"

"My cousin has a sister living with him if it interests you."

"That always interests me," I said. "You take it slow. Com'on, Chauncey."

We got back to the hotel and in bed. I was just about to get relaxed when Chauncey's voice came out of the dark from the other bed.

"Will?" he said.

I ignored him.

"Will?"

"What?"

"You feelin' better about me now, ain't'cha?"

I wanted to not answer, but I knew it was useless. "What are you talking about, Chauncey?"

"You was a little worried about me before, wadn't you? About whether or not I could handle myself."

"Chauncey, goddamnit, go to sleep." I tried to bury my head in the down pillow.

"But you feel better now, don't you?"

I didn't answer.

"I mean after the way you seen me handle that *hombre* that drew down on Chulo."

I sighed. "Oh, shit," I said.

"Did you see me move? I bet you didn't figure I was that fast, did you?"

I tried to shut his voice out. That was Chauncey. He couldn't do something good and let it lay. He had to go ahead and ruin it with his mouth.

The next night we scouted the railroad yard, staying outside the fence that enclosed it. The best I could figure there was just one night watchman. That wasn't a lot of watchdogging for a place as big as them railroad yards, but I guess they didn't figure anybody was going to just up and walk off with any of the rolling stock.

Naturally Chauncey wanted to go on in, but we had plenty of time, and I wanted to take it slow and easy. He tried to point out about where the money car would be parked on a siding, but I couldn't make out anything in the dark.

We spent the balance of that night just piddling around, taking a few drinks and looking things over. We didn't see the black Mexican, and I supposed he was keeping his horns pulled in.

I asked Chauncey: "How far down the line is this water station?"

"It's about eighty miles."

"Have you scouted it out?"

He looked surprised. "Why no! That place is a good little piece from here. Besides, what would you want to look at a watering station for? Ain't nothing there. I seen plenty of them."

"It ain't manned?"

"Oh, yeah. There'll be one water tender there, but he'll just be some old man couldn't give a baby trouble."

"Yeah," I said dryly. "Always count on that and see how far you get."

But, thinking about it, I realized I didn't have much room to be chastising Chauncey. Here I was planning on going in on a job when I knew as much about robbing trains as a pig knows about Santa Claus. Laying in bed that night I stared up in the black and wondered what it was I was doing and if I had any options.

I could go north, I thought. Go ahead until I was out of country where I was known and keep going until I outran all the wanted notices. Get a job up in the Montana or Wyoming territory working cattle or horses. Stay out of trouble and lead a nice peaceful life. Maybe find me some settler's homely daughter to marry and set up for a small rancher or trader or some such.

Yeah, I thought I could do that. Except it would be going in the opposite direction I want to go.

I tell you, the need for that woman, for Linda, was like a constant pain inside me. No matter where I was, no matter who I was with or what I was doing, she was somewhere in the back of my mind. It seemed that I wouldn't be complete until she was mine. It was a strange feeling, a sort of disconnected feeling, like half my mind and heart were somewhere else.

Yet it was so foolish. For two years that woman had tormented my mind, and what did I have to base any hopes on? A look, a word, a touch. My God, I thought, she could be married and have kids by now. Or, for sure, by the time I was able to get back and present my suit.

I was suddenly angry, angry at myself, angry at the mess I'd made of my life, angry at my foolish hopes, angry at myself for holding on to them, even angry at the woman Linda.

But mainly angry at the mess I'd made of myself.

I ought to stop this, I thought angrily. I ought to forget that damn Mexican girl. Forget this harebrained dream. I ought to go on about my business as I knew how. I ought to go and see Chulo's cousin's sister, or some other woman, any woman, and quit pining around like some schoolboy over an unreachable goddamn Mexican mirage.

I finally got so angry that I knew I wasn't going to be able to sleep. I rolled out of bed and lit the lantern and rummaged around under the bed until I found a bottle of whiskey. The light woke Chauncey up, and he opened his eyes and saw me sitting on the side of the bed drinking whiskey straight out of the bottle.

"What the hell?" he said, shading his eyes against the light. "What are you doing?"

"Go back to sleep," I said. "I don't want no company."

"What are you doing awake?"

"Goddamnit!" I said angrily. "You don't know shut up from sic 'em, do you?"

He sat up, scratching his head and yawning. "My God, Will," he said, "what do you rake me over all the time for?"

"I said I didn't want any company. And here you are settin' up to talk. Goddamnit! Go to sleep or get out of here."

My mood was very bad, though I knew, in the back of my mind, I shouldn't be taking it out on Chauncey.

He said: "You know I've heard a lot about you, Wilson. Even before I met you." His voice had an uncertain, kind of hurt sound to it that made me glance up at him. He went on. "Thing I always heard men say about you was that you was fair. They said you was a hard man, said you was dangerous, but they always said you was fair." He leaned toward me, "How come, Will, you ain't never been fair with me? You been spurrin' me from the day we met up, never givin' me no kind of chance to prove myself to you. How come you talk to me like you do?"

"Aaaaah," I said, and flipped my hand deprecatingly. I took a drink and looked down at the floor.

"How come, Will?"

"Because you're such a goddamn pup!" I said angrily. "Because you had it easy all your life. Because you got a big mouth. Because you ain't got no sense. And because I ain't got no better sense than to throw in with a pup like you on a job I ain't got no business pullin'." I took another drag on the bottle, stared down at the floor for a moment, then said: "Aw, the hell with it. I got a burr under my tail right now, and you're catching the kickin'. Why don't you go on to sleep. I'll be done here in a moment."

He didn't go to sleep, but for once, kept his mouth shut. He just sat there on the side of his bed sort of watching me. Finally I began to mellow down a little. I held the bottle toward him. "Want a drink?"

You'd of thought I was offering him a piece of bank stock the eager way he reached for that bottle. But I guess it was the first time I'd really treated him civilly.

"Thanks," he said. He took a good pull and handed me the bottle back. "Boy howdy, that lies good in a man's stomach."

"Yeah," I said. I got up and bent down and stuck my head out the window. It was a cool night for June, and I took a long breath of the good air. We were on the second floor, and I could see the lights in the big military plaza across the way. Even though it was late there was still a good bit of movement in the streets. San Antonio wasn't a town that shut up until the last drink was drunk.

I came back in the room, took another pull, then put my hand on the lamp and looked at Chauncey. "You ready for the light to go out?"

"Yeah, sure," he said. He slid down in his bed.

I turned out the light, thinking how grateful he was for the slightest kindness. I made a resolution to myself to go to treating him a little better. There was no point in me taking my irritation out on him. After all it was his money in my pocket, and, if it hadn't been for him, I'd of been riding back to Mexico with no money and no prospects.

I was pretty relaxed, what with the whiskey and blowing off a mad, and it wasn't long before I began to go to sleep. But, try as I might, I couldn't keep my mind off that girl. Finally I give it up for a bad job and just let her come again into my hopes and my dreams.

We seen the black Mexican the next day. We were taking the noon meal at a little outdoor café, and he come walking back. I give him a hail. "Hey, Chulo! You worthless greaser!"

He seen us and come over, grinning big.

"Set down and vittle up," I said.

"I eat at my cousin's," he answered. But he pulled up a chair and sat down and poured himself a glass of beer out of a pitcher we had setting on the table.

Chulo is a deceptively big man. He was taller and bigger then me, and I'm six foot and pretty solid at one hundred and eighty-five pounds. Looking at them I saw he was almost as tall as Chauncey, but a good deal wider in the shoulders and chest.

"*¿Qué pasó?*"

"Not a hell of a lot," I said. We were eating some real good *carne asada* along with some cantaloupes with lime juice squeezed on them. It was the kind of meal that fills a man up, but don't bloat him. What with the good sunshine and the beer it was a pleasant situation.

"I thought you were coming to my cousin's last night to see his sister," Chulo said.

"Where'd you get an idea like that? I never said I was coming to your cousin's. I don't even know where your cousin lives. Boy, that sister of his must be some prize the way you keep trying to run me up on her."

"She is *muy bonita*," Chulo said.

"I'll bet."

He cocked his head at me. The foam from the beer had given him a little white mustache. "Would I deceive a friend?"

"Damn right you would," I said. I finished my meal and pushed my plate back. "Quicker'n any meskin I know." I got out a little *cigarrillo,* put my feet up on a nearby chair, and lit up.

Chulo grinned. "Perhaps," he said. "But his sister is not so bad. I would take her myself except for the close blood ties."

"Hell, I'll take her!" Chauncey put in with such enthusiasm that me and the black Mexican laughed. Chauncey blushed and stammered, "That is, if Will don't want her."

Chulo looked at me. "Come tonight. My cousin's wife will make supper."

I shook my head. "Naw, me and Jesse James here got business tonight."

Chulo said "Aaaah," and Chauncey looked at me expectantly, but I didn't say anything else.

We talked awhile longer, mostly about people we knew along the border and what had become of them, and then Chulo took his leave. I poured out the last glass of beer, taking note that Chauncey still had some. He leaned across the table at me.

"What we going to do tonight, Will?"

"Look over that money car," I said, sipping at the beer. "Make sure it's like you said it would be."

"Oh, it will be," he vowed. "It will be."

I glanced at him over the top of my glass. "You're right sure about that, are you?"

"Oh, hell yes!"

"Well, it won't hurt to make sure," I said. I yawned. I was feeling better. Maybe this job would work out after all and things would go my way for once.

We went over to the railroad yard a little after one in the morning. By then the streets were pretty well deserted. It was only about half a mile, so we didn't get out horses from the livery stable, but walked. The night was about half-overcast, which made it pretty dark. When we got to the hog wire fence at the edge of the yard, we just went up a fence post and then hopped over. From there we made our way through the lines of cars, hunting for the money car.

While we hunted I asked Chauncey in a whisper, "You sure you're going to recognize this car? They all look alike to me."

"I'll know it," he said.

"How?"

"I just will. It looks— It just looks different. They got it reinforced with steel or something."

After about fifteen minutes of wandering around in the dark, Chauncey stopped me and crouched down. "That's it."

Off to our left I could see a car sided away from the others. It looked like any other baggage car, wood sided with a big sliding door in the middle.

"See the ventilation lid?" Chauncey whispered, pointing at the top of the car where a little vent hood was silhouetted against the sky.

"Hell," I whispered back, "all baggage cars got them."

"It's the one. Com'on."

We ran up to the side of the car and crouched down. After a moment I raised up and used the heel of my hand to hammer on the side. It felt solid, more so than ordinary wooden siding.

"See, it's reinforced," Chauncey said. "So you can't shoot through the siding."

"How do you get on top?" We were both still whispering though we'd spotted the watchman up at the other end of the yard.

"There's a ladder on the back," Chauncey said.

We went around to the end of the car. There was a steel ladder that went up to the top. I took a careful look around and then climbed it. I had the key to the padlock that Chauncey had given me. In the dark I fumbled around until I found the hasp and the padlock that was almost as big as my hand. In the dark I tried the key. It wouldn't fit. I tried it every way there was, but it wouldn't go in. At last I climbed down the ladder and told Chauncey.

"But it's got to," he said.

"They may have changed the lock."

"I'll see," he said, and was gone up the ladder.

He was back in a moment. "Yeah, that's a different lock. Wonder how come them to do that?"

"Let's get out of here," I said.

"Wait a minute and I'll go back up and get the name off it and we'll do like I done before."

"No," I said. I had a sinking feeling in the pit of my stomach. "Com'on." I started away in the darkness with him protesting, but following. We made it back over the fence, and I started on for the hotel.

"Will," he said. "Hey, what are we doing? We got to replace that padlock."

"No," I said, still walking.

He came up abreast. "Well, what are we going to do?"

"I don't know," I said.

I didn't say another word until we were back in the hotel. I stopped in the lobby bar to buy a bottle of whiskey and then climbed the stairs to our room. Chauncey was right behind me, about to bust, but holding it in.

I uncorked the bottle, poured out a drink, and sat down in the one chair we had.

"How come you don't want to change that padlock, Will?"

I looked up at him. "I don't like the way this looks," I said. "I don't like it at all."

"Hell, what's the hang-up?" He spread his hands. "We just do like I done before."

"Come off it," I said, a little angrily because I was worrying about the job. "Don't you see, they discovered that you'd changed that padlock and put a new one on. Don't you see they liable to be alert to some crooked doings now?"

It took him long enough, but he finally got it.

"Oh," he said. He went over and sat down on the bed.

I sat thinking and sipping at my glass of whiskey, trying to figure out how serious it was about the lock, if it blew the whole job. Finally I asked Chauncey exactly when he'd changed the lock out.

"Right after this last first of the month. Right after they got back from their run."

I thought about that, trying to decide why they would have messed with the lock anyway, with the car just sitting in the yard.

Chauncey said, "Maybe they was cleaning or something or checkin' it over, and they seen their key didn't fit, and they thought the lock was broke or messed up or something so they just changed it out."

"Yeah," I said, still thinking. I was getting that bad feeling that here was another job gone sour. It could be we'd have to call the job off.

"What you thinkin', Will?" Chauncey asked me anxiously.

I took a sip of whiskey. "I'm thinkin' I may have to find three hundred dollars somewhere to pay you back."

"Three hundred dollars? Whata you talkin' about?"

"The money you advanced me," I said. "If I pull out of the job I got to find some way to get it back to you."

"Oh," he said lowly. "I hate to hear you talk like that."

"Yeah," I said.

Finally he got up and brought a glass over. "Can I have some of that?"

I poured him out a drink, poured myself another one, and put the cork in the bottle. "I'll think about it in the morning," I said. We finished our whiskey and went to bed.

Next day I went out looking for a good horse. I'd had my mind made up as soon as I'd got my clothes on. I had to go through with the job. I had no choice. I didn't have any three hundred dollars to pay Chauncey back, nor any way of getting it. And to not do the job left me broke and stranded on the wrong side of the Rio Grande.

I'd also come to another conclusion, but I hadn't told Chauncey about that one yet. The fool had been elated when I'd told him at breakfast what we were going to do. But even as I was telling him I was marveling at why he'd want to do the job himself. He wasn't broke, and he wasn't near as wanted as I was. If he'd had any sense he'd of rode away from a holdup that was risky in the first place and that shore hadn't been helped by that lock business.

But he'd just been elated that we were going ahead. Damn fool, I'd thought, he thinks this is some kind of play game, like hares and hounds. He wants to be a big, tough train robber so he can brag in the bars and swagger down the street.

He'd said, "Well, what we going to do, replace the padlock?"

I'd shaken my head. "No, too risky. They might find it again and then the show would be up. No, we'll leave that padlock just like it is. When we do the deal we'll take a hacksaw and saw through the lock."

"Won't that take a long time?"

"We got plenty of time while that train is running that eighty miles to that water station."

"What if the clerk inside hears you sawin'?"

"The clerk ain't going to hear that with all the noise the train is making."

So we were going to do it, even though I was liking it less and less.

But I wanted that good horse, and no mistake. I hadn't let Chauncey come with me. I needed a break from his endless prattle.

I had gotten instructions at the hotel to a horse trader who was supposed to have some good stock. It was pleasant walking in the morning air, even with the little twinge of worry in the back of my mind about the job. I was keeping half an eye peeled for Chulo because I had something I wanted to talk to him about. Which was another reason I'd left the pup at the hotel. But I doubted I'd see him this early. Anyway, I figured I could ask around and get directions to his cousin's house.

I found the horse trader. He had a big barn out on Alamo Street with some horse corrals out back. He was a little, wizened up Yankee-talking type who probably got up every morning determined to show the world what a trader he was. We stood awhile in the middle of the barn, him chewing tobacco and spitting on the floor and me smoking a cigarette. I told him right off I had another horse at the livery that I reckoned to be worth forty dollars, and he said he'd have to see it, and I said it didn't really matter as I figured he wouldn't give what the horse was worth, and I'd just as soon keep him.

After we got that settled he commenced trying to sell me one of the ponies he kept in the

barn. They were all showy, cleaned up animals
that weren't at all what I had in mind. Any
horse I owned was going to see a barn damn
seldom, and I didn't want them to have any
notions about it at the start. I felt the flesh of
a few of them, and they were soft, not iron-hard
like a pony of mine needed to be. Probably good
for a lady to take a Sunday ride on, but not to
make fifty miles in a day. Meanwhile my horse
trader was carrying on about each of them,
showing me how slick and shiny their hide was
and how well their hooves were trimmed and
how this one was worth two hundred dollars
and this one a hundred and a half. I just kept
saying "Uh huh, uh huh," and waited for him
to run down. Finally I said he didn't appear to
have anything in the barn I was interested in
and maybe we might take a quick look in the
corrals outside, though I doubted I'd see what
I was looking for.

"I taken a look," I said, "when I come up, and
that's a pretty rough-looking string of horses."

He didn't agree or disagree, just kind of
looked sour and led the way out the back
door. I'd already seen a couple of ponies out
there looked like they might fit my bill, but I
wanted him to think I was more interested in
dainty horses and shiny coats.

We leaned against the fence and looked the
bunch over while he spit and I smoked. My eye
was taken by a bay gelding that looked to be
about a coming six year old. The horse was big
and rangy and didn't look to have an ounce of

fat on him. He was standing off to one side of the bunch, and I watched the way he moved around. He had a nice relaxed look about him, but the way his ears kept switching back and forth I could tell he was keeping up with what was going on. He wasn't a particularly pretty horse; his mane and tail were tangled, and he was muddy on one side. I figured he'd been a hard-using cow horse, but those long legs and the big muscled rump and hams spelled speed to me.

I signaled to the tobacco chewer let's go inside and look over the horseflesh, and we climbed through the post and rail fence and begin moving through the herd. I didn't go straight to the bay, but looked this one over and mouthed that one and generally looked dissatisfied with what I was finding. I asked a few prices, and he was quoting from a hundred up. Finally I got over to the bay and mouthed him, and he was an honest-coming six year old. While I was fooling with him I dropped my hat and flapped it in his face while I was picking it up. He jumped, but he wasn't skittish. Then I slapped him in the flanks and a few other things to see how steady he was, and he acted pretty good. He had a good gentle eye, and I liked the way he kept his head up.

After fooling around with a few other horses so the trader wouldn't get the idea I'd settled on the bay, I went back over to the fence, shaking my head.

The trader said: "Well, what's yore pick?"

I shook my head again. "I don't reckon we can trade. You don't appear to have anything to suit me. Not at the prices you've been calling."

"Why damnation, man!" he said. "You can't tell me I ain't got some stand-up hossflesh. Hell, you ain't even tried none of them."

"I don't have to ride a horse to tell if he'll suit me," I said carelessly. "Naw, I think I'll look on up the street."

"Now hold on! You ain't said a word. Make me an offer 'n see iff'en we can trade."

I acted like I was studying it over and finally asked what he'd take for a fat little roan. He asked me a hundred and a quarter.

I shook my head. "Too rich for my blood," I said. Then I nodded my head toward the bay. "What'll you take for that bay cayuse? That one looks like he's been rode hard and put up wet."

He started off to say, "Now that's a mighty fine horse—" but I cut him off with, "Naw, we're not talking about the same horse. I'm talking about that bay over in the corner there that's been rode down on somebody's cattle ranch and looks to be about a ten year old."

"Ten hell!" he said, bristling up. "That horse ain't no more than eight. And that's a fact."

I stirred my foot in the dust and looked out across town. There was a low pale of smoke hanging up in the sky from the morning cooking fires. Where I was, was kind of up on a little hill and the town looked more scattered out than it did when you were right up in it. Finally I said,

"He'd be worth seventy dollars to me."

He said, "Give me eighty-five, and it's a trade."

"Eighty," I said, "and throw in a halter and a lead rope." I didn't any more need the halter than I needed an umbrella, but that's what you do when you're trading—try and get as much as you can.

He studied about it a moment and finally said he believed we could trade. I was pleased. I'd sort of planned on going at least a hundred and a quarter on the horse if I'd had to because I wanted him and knew he'd make me a good mount.

Later, walking to the livery stable leading my new horse, I reflected on what I'd just done. I'd haggled and bargained and schemed over a few dollars just as if it was as important as any job I'd pulled. What's more, I'd enjoyed myself. It was, I thought, a sad conclusion to come to that I enjoyed honest business as much as I did outlaw work when I was so knee-deep in the latter. But I'd made my choices, and now I was going to have to live with them. A man had to play the cards he was dealt, but it seemed wrong somehow that a man made so many selections that applied to the rest of his life when he was so damn young he didn't have good sense.

I put my horse up at the livery stable, sold my old horse to the man that ran the place for thirty-five dollars, and I felt like I'd had a good morning. I still needed to talk to Chulo.

I had resolved to get his reaction before I told Chauncey what I planned. Accordingly, I went up to the plaza and looked around in the various saloons and cafés, but Chulo wasn't up and about. I figured I'd catch him around noontime.

CHAPTER 4

We were sitting in the formal room of his cousin's house, Chulo and I. We'd had a good supper of *cabrito* and beans and rice. I didn't know where Chulo's cousin and the cousin's wife had got off to, but they'd vanished. The cousin's sister had brought us a bottle of whiskey and a pitcher of water and some glasses, and then she, too, had withdrawn.

The sister wasn't bad. She was pretty in the way some of them Mexican gals are though she was getting a little plump. I reckoned her to be around twenty-two or twenty-three years of age. She didn't talk much, but the cousin had told me she'd been married to a young man in Mexico who'd been killed on a horse-stealing raid into Texas. Since then she'd been living with him and his wife. Looking at her during the meal, seeing her breasts and her soft lips and the way her lips swelled, I'd felt my neck starting to thicken and the old familiar copperish taste come into my mouth. It had been a long time since I'd had a woman, and

I was near froze for the feel of one.

But I had business. We sat and smoked and drank awhile, letting our supper digest, and then I told Chulo I wanted to talk to him about a job.

He looked up at me, his face circled in the blue smoke from his *cigarrillo*, and raised his eyebrows.

"It ain't exactly the kind of job you been used to, but it might turn out to be a pretty fair takin'." I didn't know quite where to begin. "And it might be a little risky," I said.

Chulo is a hell of a kidder in a dry way. He wrinkled up his brow and said, "Risky? You mean *ten cuidado*? Well, señor, I tell you, I've never done anything, how you say, risky!"

"Aw, go to hell," I said. Finally I just laid it out for him the best I understood it myself. I wound up by saying, "The kid thinks we'll get forty thousand in gold. I think he knows, but I ain't sure. Anyway, it never felt like no two-man job to me, and, since I found out they'd changed that padlock back, I know it ain't no two-man job. I don't want to jump down in that car by myself and find four armed guards. I need somebody with me."

Chulo half-smiled. "Ah, yes, I understand that. You would prefer we both get killed than you solo. A very good thought."

"Come'on," I said. "I ain't planning on nobody getting killed, but I've had all the surprises I want in this robbery business. Probably it will be just that one clerk, because, like Chauncey says, I believe they depend on secrecy to get that money through. Anyway, you're about the best man I know of, and you're here and I thought I'd proposition you about it." I trailed off and leaned back in my chair and poured myself a glass of whiskey with a little water in it. While Chulo smoked and thought, I looked around. The house was bigger than most and pretty well furnished. The walls were adobe with a thick coat of plaster. There was a little altar against a far wall with a statue of the Virgin Mary and a burning candle.

The black Mexican finally said, "And I'm to jump into that car with you?"

"Yeah," I said. "I figure that's where the worst trouble will come. I expect the kid can handle the water tender. At least I hope he can."

"I don't much like it," Chulo said. "Jumping down in there."

"I know," I admitted. "I don't like it either." I hadn't told him about the oily rags, which was the best protection I'd been able to think of.

Chulo blew out a cloud of smoke. "Robbing a train. Of the bank's money. In Texas." He shook his head. "Ah, Chiushaha!"

"I know. But it's better than ten thousand a man. And that's a pretty good payday."

"I think the peoples we steal the money from will be very angry."

"I believe you're right," I said. Chulo was a hell of a gun, and I needed him, but I wasn't going to push him.

"I think they chase the hell out of us."

"I bet they do," I said.

He shook his head again. "Already I'm wanted in Mexico for robbing a Mexican bank. Now I will commit a robbery in Texas and be wanted here. Where can I go, *amigo*?"

"Canada?" I suggested.

"Brrrrr," he said. "Too cold."

I let him think awhile longer, keeping quiet. He asked, "You think it's forty thousand?"

I shrugged. "That's what the kid says. And he seems pretty sure." I told him about Chauncey advancing me the three hundred dollars.

Finally Chulo said, "Well, why the hell not. How long can a man live, anyway."

We had a drink to seal the bargain, and then Chulo stood up. "Let's go to a saloon and raise a little hell."

I glanced toward the door the sister had disappeared through. "I believe," I said, "I'll just sit here awhile."

Chulo looked amused. "You think you will sit here awhile." He laughed. "I will tell her you are waiting on my way out."

"Yeah," I said, feeling my throat getting tight again.

We said our adióses and Chulo left, leaving me sitting, waiting, and drinking whiskey. I tell you, I was ready.

She came in about ten minutes and sat in the chair next to me, her hands folded modestly in her lap. In Spanish I told her what a good supper it had been and asked if she'd had a large hand in fixing it.

"Yes," she said, hesitantly. "*Todas*."

"Ah, you fixed it all. Well, it was very good." I felt awkward with the woman for some reason. Awkward and uneasy. I guess it was because it had been so long. I didn't quite know what to do or say. The woman was not a *puta*, a whore, yet she would make herself available to the right man. Because she had been married there was no longer a question of her purity, and her brother was under no obligation to protect it. It was customary with such a woman to give her money, but you gave it as a gift, not a payment as you would with a *puta*.

She looked very unconcerned about the whole situation. I guessed she'd been through it enough that she pretty well knew what was expected.

I poured myself out another drink, looking at her while I did, wishing she'd speak or do something. I finally downed my drink and went to her and lifted her up by the shoulders and kissed her. She responded docily, participating in the kiss enough to tell me that she was agreeable to what was to come next, but not enough so that she could be said to be excited. Still standing I kept one arm around her waist and used my other hand to undo the buttons of her bodice. When it was open enough so that I could get my hand in I stroked her breasts, surprised at how white they were against the parts of her body that were not covered. The nipples were very rosy and began to be hard as I stroked them. Still holding her I leaned down and kissed her breasts. Then I was going to unbutton her bodice farther, but she took my hand and shook her head.

"Let us go to my room," she said.

I followed her out of the formal room, she leading me by the hand, and into the darkness of a hall. She opened a door, and we went into a dimly lit room, lit only by the candle at the little altar that was against the wall. Once in she went to the side of the bed and then turned to face me, dropping her hands to her sides. My breath was coming fast and hard, and my hands were shaking as I tried to unbutton her dress all the way down. Finally she took the task into her own fingers, motioning for me to undress as she did.

When she was down to her underclothes she got in bed and modestly finished undressing under the covers. But it did her no good. As soon as I was naked I threw the coverings back and looked at her. She wanted to cover herself with her hands, but I pulled them back and buried my face in her warm, soft belly. She smelled good; healthy and clean and good. I crawled up on top of her, hurrying because I wanted to be inside of her before it was too late. She seemed to understand my urgency and helped me as best she could. Then I could smell her and feel her and taste her. It went quickly.

Her name was Cata. She came from Durango, in Mexico, obviously from a good class family. She said she was twenty-two. Other than that and the business about her husband being killed, I knew nothing more about her when I got ready to leave in the morning. She came to me before I was up, bringing me coffee and a pear. She looked the same as she had before I'd slept with her; looking at me in the same way, saying the same things, casting her eyes the same way. Strangely enough I thought what we had done should have wrought a change in her, made her see me differently. But while I drank my coffee I wondered why I should think so. I guessed it was because I seen her differently.

When she came back to take the eating things I pulled her down in the bed with me, and, without taking her clothes off, except for her undergarments, I just threw her dress up and had her again. I was not tender, even a little rough. I guessed it was because she had disappointed me, coming in the next morning and still acting like the same dumb cow. Well, if she wanted to act like a piece of baggage, I'd treat her like one.

But then I was ashamed. She was gone when I got up to dress, and I put ten dollars under her pillow. It was too much, but then my need had been great and I was ashamed for being angry because I'd expected her to act like something she wasn't. I knew who I wanted her to remind me of.

I got to the hotel in time to catch Chauncey having breakfast in the dining room. I dropped into a chair and ordered steak and eggs from the waiter who came hurrying up.

"Goddamn," Chauncey said, "you been out all night. You didn't come in last night."

"You're a mighty observant boy," I said dryly. I felt good; relaxed and confident.

"Where the hell was you?"

"Out fucking," I said briefly.

"Out— Say what!"

"Out fucking, Chauncey. You know, what men and women do when it works out."

"Who with?" he blurted out.

"Now, Chauncey, be a good lad and don't ask so many goddamn questions. Besides, I got some business to talk with you."

Chauncey didn't take the news about Chulo very well when I told him up in the room. But I was patient with him, reminding myself that it was, after all, his job.

"Hell!" he said, getting to his feet when I told him. "What'd you go and do something like that for? And who told you you could go and do something like that!"

"It was necessary," I said briefly.

"Well, I'd like to know who, by God, decided that?"

"Take it easy, Chauncey," I said. "You haven't heard me out."

He said, "Well, you better have a damn good reason," and dropped down on his bed, giving me an outraged look.

I almost wanted to laugh at his presumptions, but I check reined myself. "Well, I don't know how good it is," I said mildly. "As a matter of fact we don't have to take Chulo in at all. Not if you want to drop into that car by yourself after they've discovered that the padlock has been changed. In fact, if that's agreeable to you, I'll go and tell him right now. I'm sure I can handle that water tender by myself." I made as if to get up, doing it slowly so he'd have time to understand what I'd said.

"Wait a minute," he said. "What's that got to do with it?"

"Just that I ain't dropping into that car by myself where there might be four or five guns waiting for me. I'm a coward and I want some help with me. But if it won't bother you then I'm all for leaving Chulo out of it."

He thought about it a minute and then started whining. "But that means we got to split the money three ways. You didn't promise him a full share, did you?"

"No," I said, "I didn't promise him a full share. In fact the subject never came up. But since he's taking the same risks I am I *assume* he figures to get the same split."

"But hell, Will," he protested. "It's my plan. I ought to get at least half."

"Oh, you don't want half," I said. "You want it all. Tell you what, why don't you go ahead and take all of it. Look at it as a one man job."

"Aw, don't start that old stuff again," he said, looking unhappy and dejected. "I just don't see why we need to split the money up."

"Don't think about the money, Wild Bill," I said, "think about the glory. Ain't that what you're in this for, the glory of being a big, tough train robber?"

I was about half-disgusted with him, but he finally quit whining and acted like he about half-understood why we had to have another gun on the job. He hadn't made any gains in my estimation by his attitude, however.

On the twentieth of the month we saddled our horses, rolled our sleeping bags, and set out overland to have a look at the watering station. Chauncey thought it was a lot of trouble for nothing and appeared to be set to complain about it the whole way.

But Chulo said: "Listen, my young friend, you don't expect no thing to be very easy in this business. It is better to look into the holes of all the groundhogs."

"Yeah," Chauncey said, "but this is going to take three or four days. And who wants to be out in this godforsaken country when we could be back in town. Hell, one water station's like another. I thought you two was supposed to be such big-time outlaws and here you are making a fuss about a goddamn water station. Shit!"

I'd heard all I wanted to hear. I reined my horse up and took Chauncey's by the rein so he couldn't ride by. "Listen," I told him flatly, "I've heard all this bitching and whining and playing the calf out of you I'm going to put up with. You pull the bad mouth once more on this trip, and I'm going to whip you till the taste runs out of your mouth. I am sick and tired of your shit.

This job is going to be bad enough without you acting the crybaby. Now you act like a man or pay the consequences." I let go his bridle and turned and rode off without another look.

I knew it was pretty hard on him, me shaming him like that in front of Chulo. All the time I'd been reading him out he'd just sat his horse, not saying a word, while the fear had come into his face. Well, I felt a little bad about it, but goddamnit, he'd brought it on himself, and a man ought not to get mouthy unless he can back it up.

Chulo came up beside me. I glanced over my shoulder. Chauncey was hanging back, his head down.

Chulo said: "Tomorrow we come into some pretty country, I thenk."

"I thenk so, too," I said, mocking him.

Chulo grinned, but his thoughts were on something else. He jerked his head backward. "He is very much the *niño*, eh?"

I frowned. "Yeah, he acts like a boy."

Chulo said: "That's not too good. What you thenk, eh?"

I hesitated, choosing my words carefully. I didn't want to try and lie to Chulo, because it wouldn't fool him in the first place. But I could tell that Chauncey was worrying him, and I wanted to think of something to say that would set his mind at ease. I couldn't afford for Chulo to pull out of the job.

"Look, Chulo," I said, "I know how it looks to you. I admit the kid ain't much. But his part ain't very important. All he's got to do is hold a watering station long enough for us to get off the train. A fool ought to be able to do that."

Chulo said, dryly, "Well, it looks like you've picked the right man for the job."

"Aw, com'on, Chulo," I said, "Chauncey ain't that bad. Look, if he was to have an important part in this job I'd be worried about it, too. In fact I'd of never taken the job on in the first place. But, God, I know he can handle an unguarded water station!"

"Perhaps," Chulo said lowly. "Perhaps."

We rode slowly, taking our time, stopping to make a leisurely meal along a sparkling little creek. I was liking my new horse damn well. They'd slicked him up at the livery stable, and he'd turned into a fine-looking animal. But, more important, he'd proven to be a first-class mount with speed and, I hoped, staying power. I intended to find the latter out on the ride down and back. Accordingly, that afternoon I pushed the pace up, explaining that I wanted to be in a position to strike the water station before noon the next day.

Chauncey was still sulking, but the Negro and I paid him no mind. We were starting to get into what they called the hill country, bunches of little hills, four and five hundred feet high cut with gullies and washouts and everywhere covered with cedar and mesquite and granite and limestone rocks. It looked to me to be the beginning of a country a man could hide out in pretty well. It was for sure he wasn't going to be spotted a long way off, not the way the land was cut up.

Late in the afternoon we passed Devine, taking a route around it even though Chauncey had the audacity to venture the opinion that we ought to go in for a drink.

I started to tongue-lash him again, but ended up saying, "Naw, I don't want us seen down in this country."

Devine was forty miles out of San Antonio, and I figured we went on another ten miles before making camp. That give us fifty miles on the day, and my horse had stood up just fine. Of course the others had too. Which was only as it had to be. There was no use in one mount being better than the others when you were running from a job because you're only going as far and as fast as the poorest animal will take you.

We were now at the base of the hills. To the south the rolling plains stretched out as far as the eye could see. Dilley, the closest town to the watering station, was another thirty miles ahead. We wouldn't make it before noon, but we'd be there early enough in the afternoon to have our look and be well back on the road to San Antonio before dark. And, going back, I wanted to take a different route. I had a plan in mind that I wanted to check into and see how good it might pan out.

In spite of what Chauncey had said, it was good to be sleeping outdoors. A man didn't want it as a steady diet, but it was might fine once in a while in good weather.

After we'd had chuck we built the fire up a little and ranged ourselves around it on our saddles and bedrolls. I lit a *cigarrillo* and smoked and looked up at the star stung sky. After a time, I said, "Hey, Negro!"

"*Díga me, amigo.*" He was laying off to my right. We'd grained the horses and then picketed them out where they could get a little grazing off the poor ground.

"I was wondering," I said, "how you got in this business. What was your first job?"

I heard Chulo laugh. "Well, you ask the hard question, *amigo*. It would not be possible for me to remember my first act of thievery it has been so long."

"Well, what was the first one you remember?"

"Let me thenk," he said. Then: "It was when me and my two brothers robbed a butcher shop in Chicahua City one night when it was closed. We broke in the back, and I remember that the beef carcass we stole was almost too heavy for us to carry." He chuckled dryly. "That was, I believe, my first adventure into the business of stealing cattle."

"Well when did you pretty much know you were set on the business of stealing for a living?" It was worthless, idle talk, but we were all relaxed and comfortable, and it was a time for such prattle.

"Oh, no, my friend," Chulo said quickly, "I never made any such plans to go into it as one chooses the profession of a lawyer or a doctor.

I just drifted into it out of the necessity of our poor circumstances, and very shortly it was too late. I was on a road that had no turning."

"Yeah," I said, suddenly depressed by the clarity with which he'd said it. I too was on a road with no turning. "Yeah, that's about me. Man gets in it and thinks just one more job, just one more, just one more. And pretty soon it's too late. He's wanted and his crimes have reached the point where his capture would mean the rest of his life. Yes, I understand that very well."

Of course Chauncey had to throw his rope in. There was still a touch of the sulkiness in his voice. "Hell, I don't see where it's such a bad life. Either one of you'd had to work as hard as I've had to all my life, first on a farm and then tending to goddamn cattle, you wouldn't be complaining about it. It's going to suit me damn well, you betcha."

"You wait, *niño*," Chulo said quietly. "Perhaps you will have a changing of the mind."

We broke camp early, taking time only for coffee and some cold biscuits we'd brought from the hotel. Going over the plains was pretty easy riding, and we made good time right from the start. We had been cutting overland for the most part of the journey, but now we began to drift over to pick up the railroad tracks.

We rode hard the balance of the forenoon, but we stopped and made a good meal when the sun was high. I figured we couldn't be much short of the watering station, though it was hard to tell in that country. Wadn't a damn thing to use for a distance marker. I reckoned that extreme south Texas was some of the most unpopulated country in the nation. We hadn't even seen very many cattle. But, then, that shouldn't have been surprising, as poor as the land was. Land like that couldn't run many cattle.

It felt strange riding with Chulo and Chauncey. I hadn't ridden with partners since Les and Tod, and I'd ridden with them so long that it seemed unnatural to be riding with anyone else. I guess it was about like being married to a woman for a long time and then living with another one. You kept expecting the new one to have the ways of the old one that you were so accustomed to.

About an hour after nooning we raised the big water tower out of the horizon. We kept on in good style, making our way through the thick mesquite and underbrush until we were right up to the clearing around the station. It wasn't much; just that water tower with its big arm of a spigot that they let down to fill the train's boilers, and a shack with a horse corral in back. There were a couple of sorry-looking cayuses in the corral standing around switching flies in the afternoon sun. It had gotten considerably hotter since we'd come down out of the hill country and hit the low plains. We didn't see anybody moving around the station so we sat our horses and watched for a while. Finally I got off my horse and led him a few feet back into the mesquite thicket. The others followed suit.

"Chauncey," I said, "you go on up there and see what's going on. Make like you're heading onto Mexico and have just stopped to water your horse. Find out how many men are on duty and when. But don't give it away, you understand. Be careful and don't let anybody there get the idea you're scouting the place out."

He looked insulted. "In spite of what you might think, Mr. Big-Time Outlaw, I ain't exactly a idjet!"

He got on his horse and rode toward the station. Chulo and I watched him. I said, "Well, I'm afraid that I'm not that boy's idol anymore."

Chulo laughed. We made ourselves comfortable in what shade we could find and waited for Chauncey to return. I'd sent him in because it would be he who would be taking the station, and I wanted him to have a look at the place. But I'd also sent him because I figured he needed pumping up a little.

It took Chauncey about three quarters of an hour to get back because he had to leave the station on the south side, to support his story that he was going to Mexico, then make a wide loop, keeping out of sight, and back around to us. He rode up looking disgusted. As he got off his horse he said: "All this long ride for nothing!"

"How's that?"

He jerked a hand in the direction of the water station. "They ain't nobody there but one old man. And he's about half-gimpy."

"What are you complaining about?" Chulo asked him quietly. "Would you have preferred there had been a squadron of *regulares* stationed there?"

"Aw, it's just—" he said. He gave me a look. "I told *everybody* that we didn't need to make this trip, that one water station is the same as another. But no, we had to make this long trip down here. For one old man that's about as dangerous as a suckling pig."

"Take it easy, Chauncey," I said.

"Aw, shit!" he said. "I'll be glad when somebody around this outfit goes to trusting me."

"Shut up, Chauncey." I said it with a pause before his name, because, for one instant I'd almost called him Tod. Which made me sweat a little, for Tod had always been bad luck. And even though Chulo is a good man, he's not a Les, and having a Tod without a Les to balance him off was a bad bargain indeed. I tried to put it out of my mind, him reminding me of Tod. It's sometimes bad luck to think about bad luck.

We took a more westerly route going back, which was longer and much rougher traveling, but I was doing it for a reason.

As we traveled through the gullies and bluffs of the hill country I was constantly keeping my eyes open for a good place to lay up maybe a week or two after the robbery. I hadn't said anything to the others, but I'd got to thinking that after we'd robbed a train of bank gold we'd be more in demand by the law than a whore in a cow camp. It wouldn't be smart to lay around ordinary haunts in Texas, and I figured they'd be watching and patrolling the border for at least a week, figuring us to break for there. So what I'd thought we'd do was to hole up in really rough country until things had cooled down a bit.

I was trying to hit the town of Bandera. It was a little village back in the rough country set along the Guadalupe River. It had been founded as a shingle town, the shakes and shingles being cut out of the big cypress trees that grew along the river. But when that industry cratered it had somehow managed to hold on. On what I didn't know. Of course it wasn't much; couple of stores, including a saloon, and a blacksmith. There was no law, of that I was sure. And the remaining citizens were a pretty hard lot. Not the kind that would be asking too many questions of strangers for fear that they might get asked some questions themselves.

I had a pretty good idea of where it was, but in that country so much of it looks alike that a man can't be sure. But pretty soon we topped a little bluff and there was Bandera.

"Well, boys," I said, "what say we go in and have a drink."

"¿Cómo no?" Chulo said, and we put spurs to our horses and rode on into town, pulling up in front of the saloon. It was a little rock building that did double duty as a mercantile and grocery. We tied our horses and went on in. The barkeep, such as he was, was dozing at one of the three rough-hewn tables he had setting there. He woke up when he seen us.

"Yes, sir, yes sir!" he said, bustling behind the bar and looking ready. "What'll it be, gents?"

"Whiskey all around," I said, "best you got."

He got out a bottle of common pop skull and poured us a drink all around. "Here's to luck," I said.

"Luck," Chauncey said.

"*Suerte*," Chulo said.

We knocked the whiskey off, taking it down fast to avoid the taste. The barkeep poured us out another one. We took our drinks and went over to a table.

"How does this suit you?" I asked them.

The two of them looked at me questioningly, and I told them what I'd been planning, how we'd jump up here after the robbery instead of breaking for the border as they'd be expecting us to.

"See," I said, "from the watering station it's still one hundred and twenty miles to the border, and we'd never make that in two or three days. That would give John Law time to telegraph down there, and you can bet there'd be plenty of patrols out and all the bridges tied up tight."

Chulo nodded, seeing the sense in it.

"So," I said, "what we do is break up to this country. About a eighteen-mile ride. 'Course we don't stay in the town here, that'd be too risky.

We'll make us a camp about a mile out or so in one of these hidden canyons."

Chauncey said, in a voice a little too loud for secrecy, "Hell, I don't want to live like no fuckin' Indian or nigger for two weeks. Shit!"

"Keep your goddamn voice down!" I said, getting irritated.

"Well, I just don't see the sense of it," Chauncey insisted, though he did lower his voice.

Chulo said, "It is a good plan, my young friend. After we make that robbery there will be many gennelmens of the law looking for us. No, I thenk we had better listen to El Capitán. He knows."

"El Capitán, huh!" Chauncey said. "Who the hell elected him?"

He was really getting uppity. I figured I was going to have to have a nice quiet little talk with him.

Chulo said: "He is the best, that is the reason." Then he said, very levelly, "And if I am willing to accept that, surely you—"

He let it hang, his meaning plenty clear.

About that time a man come through the front door, and I said, "Let's let it lay."

The man was wearing run-over boots and a dirty shirt and pants, but he had a large caliber revolver strapped to his right hip. He was chewing tobacco, and he spit on the floor while he ordered a drink from the bartender. There was about a six-day growth of beard on his face, and his hair was long and unkept.

He turned at the bar to study us, shifting his cud back and forth in his mouth as he looked us over.

I figured the way he was making himself free with the place that he was from close around and a regular customer. I didn't want any trouble with the home folks, not if we were to hide out in the place, and this one looked like a mean cuss. He spit on the floor again.

"Hey!" Chauncey suddenly said, calling to the man. "Was you raised in a pigpen?"

The man turned slowly around and stared at us, trying to see who it was that had spoken. He stopped chewing. I was trying to think of something to say or do when Chauncey said:

"Didn't yore mamma teach you not to spit on the floor?"

The man looked puzzled more than angry. I reached around and told Chauncey, almost hissing: "Shut up, goddamnit, fool! Shut up!" Then I looked at the man at the bar. "No offense, *hombre*," I said. I jerked my head at Chauncey. "He's drunk."

Chauncey started to protest that he wasn't drunk, but Chulo took him by the shoulder and shook him.

"No offense," I said again to the man. Then I got up and got a wad of Chauncey's shirtfront and started leading him out the door. Chulo pitched a couple of silver dollars on the bar and helped me get Chauncey out of the door. We were holding him so tight he couldn't make a fuss. But, once at the horses, he began to protest. "Goddamn, Will, what you mean dragging me out of that place? You can't treat me like this!"

"Get on that horse!" I said. I was so mad I was having trouble talking, my jaws were clenched so tight. "Get on that horse before I beat you to death."

He seen I meant it and slowly mounted. But he was still mouthing. "I still didn't see where you get off draggin'—"

"Shut up!" I said. "Shut up!"

After we were out of town and had ridden a ways I began to cool down. "Look, fool," I said, speaking as if I were talking to a child, "that was the place we were going to hide out. You may have messed it up. Chauncey, you don't shit in your own nest. We didn't want to call attention to ourselves, and now you not only have called attention to us you have made an enemy. And that man you was giving a lesson in manners to is from around there."

"How you know that?" he asked me defiantly.

"Just take his word for it," Chulo suddenly put in. I could hear anger in his voice. "Just believe Wilson. He is experienced. You are not!"

Chauncey wouldn't let it lie, nor would he learn. "But he was spitting on the floor!"

I just looked over at Chulo and shook my head. He made no sign, but he looked thoughtful.

Now there wasn't much to do except hang around San Antonio and wait for the end of the month. Chauncey was still acting sulky in spite of my having a talk with him. I couldn't figure out why, but he sure seemed to resent Chulo being part of the job. I guess me taking on Chulo without consulting him had made him feel that the job wasn't just all his baby anymore. That or something else. Hell, I couldn't figure the boy out, and I'd gotten tired of trying. I just figured to keep him in line until we'd made the money off that train job and get shut of him.

I'd kind of got a little more confident about the job since I'd done a little work on it. If the gold was there and it all went the way it should, we wouldn't have too much to worry about.

We did have one more chore to do after we got back from scouting the water station. Me and Chulo loaded up a bunch of canned goods, tomatoes and apricots and beef, along with some saltines and some salt pork and went and located us a camp that would do for a hideout. We decided on a place about a mile and a half out of Bandera, and it was a good one. It was at the base of a bluff that started down in this little gully. Obviously water had once in a while come racing through the gully because the limestone of the bluff had been cut back some six feet at the bottom, leaving a shelf or a ledge that made a natural shelter. It was about five feet high and about forty feet long as well as, as noted, about six feet deep. It made a good fort. Nobody was going to get at you from the back or from overhead, and there was a line of boulders on the other side of the gully that gave you protection from that side. I sure didn't want to have to do it, but it would be a handy place to defend.

We'd also packed in ten gallons of water. We didn't expect to have to use it, for there was a spring located not more than a half a mile away. But if we were to get pinned down the water might be the saving of us.

Though I was still a little nervous about being a wanted man in San Antonio, no attention had been paid to me. San Antonio is an unusual town in that a wanted man can feel fairly safe there from the local law if he behaves himself. The local law don't seem to much care what you've done somewhere else so long as you don't cause them any trouble. 'Course that don't mean you don't have to watch for outside law who might come to town. In fact they might come in looking for somebody else, and it could just be your hard luck that they see you first.

The waiting got pretty monotonous and I developed the habit, of an evening, of going over and seeing Cata. I finally rented a cheap hotel room for a week so I could take her out of the house. It had got pretty uncomfortable coming into the formal room and greeting the cousin and his wife and squirming around until I could find a way to slip off to the back bedroom with Cata. It was like saying, "Good evening, sir and madame. How are you this evening? Now if you'll excuse me I've come here to fuck your sister."

That sounds exaggerated, but that's about the way it felt. Worse, that's about the way it worked out.

I'd quit giving her ten dollars. That was getting a little expensive considering the regularity we were going at it. And then a curious thing happened about the third evening we went to the hotel. I was in the habit of slipping money under the pillow while her back was turned and then putting on my clothes and leaving, letting her take her departure at the most likely moment.

But that evening, as I was leaving the room, she called out to me. I turned and she was holding the five-dollar gold piece I'd left. She looked very shy, but she said, looking away from me, *"Por favor, por favor."*

I took a step back toward her not understanding. *"¿Qué pasa?"*

"No guiro," she said, still looking away.

She didn't want it? I didn't understand what was the matter. For a second I thought she didn't want it because she didn't think it was enough, but then she said, *"No más dinero, por favor."*

That confused me even more, so I sat down on the bed to talk with her as best I could. There was no language barrier to speak of, but there was her shyness and my inability to talk in the right, polite way. But what it finally came down to was that she didn't want to take any more money from me. She was perfectly willing to come to the hotel with me so long as I was in town, but she didn't want any more money.

I was astounded. I didn't know what to think, much less what to say. But, sitting there, I began to realize I'd already noticed some little changes in her. She kissed me different, for one thing. Oh, she wasn't any more passionate, but she'd begun to kiss me longer and with more feeling, I guess I'd call it. And then she seemed to smile more. And I'd noticed the way she watched me when I was undressing or when I was walking around the room.

I didn't know what to make of it, but she acted about like she was starting to feel a little tender toward me.

I didn't know that I liked that. It had been all right when she made herself available to me and I gave her money. That seemed a square deal, one that I could understand. But here was this new thing. She was doing what I'd had a few whores do with me, refuse my money, and say, "No, we fuck for love."

That was all right with whores because you knew it wadn't going to go no further. But Cata wasn't no whore, and I didn't want her gettin' any ideas. So far as women were concerned I had my plans already made. And, as bad as it sounds, I didn't consider that Cata stood in there so far as my ideas of quality were concerned.

Besides that, as close as we were to the job, I didn't want no woman cluttering up my thinking. I wanted my mind free and dedicated to the job at hand. A man in my line of work has got to strain his mind to allow for every eventuality and be prepared to take care of it somehow.

And then, a week before the job, Chauncey got himself arrested.

CHAPTER 5

It wasn't any use blaming Chauncey. He hadn't made himself any more free-er around town as a wanted man than I had. He'd just been less lucky. He'd walked into a saloon where an out-of-town law, from the same locale as Chauncey's daddy-in-law, had been having his last drink before hitting the trail south. He'd recognized Chauncey, known he was wanted, and had jerked him over to the calaboose under arrest.

Of course we didn't know that right away, only learned it later when we were able to get an emissary in to talk to Chauncey.

I got the word by accident at the hotel from the clerk who didn't know a thing about it, only that Chauncey had been arrested. I'd hunted up Chulo and we went to the little outside café down by the river walk and sat there, over a pitcher of beer, trying to think what to do.

Chulo was in favor of going ahead with the job without Chauncey. But I shook my head. "We can't do that, Negro. It's his job. We can't cut him out of it."

"But you know as much of it now as he does. It is the job of the man with the information."

I shook my head again. "Can't do it, Chulo. It ain't my style."

He poured himself a glass of beer, waiting until the foam settled before saying anything. It was a nice afternoon, sunny and bright, but not hot. They had a parrot in a cage who was imitating the owner calling a cat. Over and over he called, "Kitty, kitty, kitty, here kitty." Then he'd laugh. I'd seen the cat come running any number of times to the parrot's call. He'd come jumping eagerly into the patio, looking for the owner and whatever she had to feed him, then stand around looking puzzled while the parrot laughed his head off. The cat never did snap to the parrot calling him.

"I thenk," Chulo said thoughtfully, "it would be an easier job for just us of the two. I do not thenk we must have two in the car. One would be *bastante*. You could go in the car, or I—as you choose. The other would be for the *estación de agua*."

"That ain't it, Chulo. You know it ain't. Like I said, it's Chauncey's job, and we can't go ahead without him." I was feeling pretty low about things, but I meant what I was telling Chulo.

"But that is not practical," Chulo protested. "We have made plans, and we have invested time."

"I can't help it, Chulo," I said doggedly. "I won't go ahead with the job with Chauncey in jail. And that's final. And God knows I need the money worse than anybody I can think of. But I just won't do it, no matter what kind of punk Chauncey is."

Chulo opened his hands. "Then what are we to do?"

I hesitated, knowing how silly my words were going to sound. "Well," I finally said, "we got to see if we can't get Chauncey out of jail."

"Ha ha ha," Chulo laughed dryly. "No thank you very much, *amigo*. This is one meskin who is not robbing any jails in San Antonio, Texas." He pulled his big, blue steel revolver out of its holster and idly spun the chamber with his thumb. He carried a straight Colt's caliber .44. The newest improved navy model. I didn't like the gun. I thought it had too much power to make for accurate shooting. I carried a .44/.40, which was a .40 caliber on a .44 frame. That way I had the weight of the frame along with enough power to get the job done, but not enough to make for inaccurate shooting. It would generally hit whatever I pointed it at. Chulo's and mine were both double-action revolvers, but we never fired them that way. Pulling the hammer back by pulling the trigger caused just enough barrel deflection to spoil your shot.

"I know that," I said. "I'm not interested in breaking him out of jail myself. But what we need right now is some information. I don't even know what he's charged with. You and I can't go, but we got to get somebody in that jail to talk to him and find out what's going on."

"My cousin," Chulo said.

"Your cousin?" I wasn't so sure about that. I knew his cousin dealt in stolen cattle and horses, and I didn't know how welcome he'd be around the jailhouse. "I don't know about your cousin, Negro. He goes up to the jail they're liable to keep him."

Chulo laughed. "My cousin is a man of influence with the calaboose authorities. He has many friends among the guards and jailers. If anyone can get the information you seek, it is my cousin."

Which was the way it worked out. He met us next afternoon in the café after an early morning visit to the jail. Chulo's cousin was a fat, perspiring man named Gustino. Chulo called him Gordo, which means fat in Mexican.

We observed the formalities and drank a couple of glasses of beer before Gordo talked.

"It is hot, no?" he said, taking out a big white silk handkerchief and mopping his brow.

"Yeah," I said, not agreeing because it wasn't hot, but hoping to hurry him along to telling us what he'd found out.

He finally told us about Chauncey being recognized by the law from his daddy-in-law's stomping grounds and being taken into custody and lodged in the local jail. But then he gave us some very interesting information. He said: "Thes marshal from Laredo is going to take cho frieen back to the border in four days' time. He is going to take him on horseback over across the country."

"The hell you say!" I exclaimed. He went on talking, and we found out that the local sheriff was short on space in the jail and wanted this Laredo marshal to get Chauncey the hell out of there. The marshal couldn't produce any paper to show that Chauncey was wanted, and the sheriff didn't want to fool with it. So the marshal was going to set out in four days with Chauncey on horseback. Was going by himself because he didn't figure Chauncey had any friends here, and it wouldn't be any trouble.

Well, that was just pie for us. For sure me and Chulo could rob a town marshal of one prisoner. I looked over at Chulo. "Ain't but one road out of here, *amigo*."

"*Sí*," he said, but he didn't look very happy about it.

I asked Gordo to keep us posted on the plans, gave him twenty dollars to sweeten up his informant, and felt like things weren't as black as they had been. After the cousin was gone, I said to Chulo, "Let's get another pitcher of beer and think this out."

"Sure," he said, but he was smoking meditatively.

"What's the matter, Chulo?" I asked him.

"Nothing," he said. "*Nada.*"

"Com'on, Chulo."

He ground his cigarette out and shrugged meditatively. "I don't like that *niño*," he said flatly. "And if I don't like him, why should I trouble myself to keep him from jail?"

"Because the job depends on it," I said. "Hell, I don't like him either."

"There are other jobs," Chulo said carelessly. "Which are less trouble."

"Look," I said, "this has got to be done. There's no other way."

He shrugged. "It is becoming very complicated, I thenk."

I sat back and looked at him. His black face was impassive under his wide-brimmed hat. "Chulo," I said, "I've got to do it. I got no choice. Now, you going to help me?"

He glanced at me, holding a *cigarrillo* near his mouth, one boot up on a nearby table. Finally he pulled a face. "Well, if you got to do it I thenk I will help you. Though you are a fool."

"I ain't no stranger to being a fool," I said. I hunched forward over the table. "Now what we got to do is saddle up tomorrow and take us about a ten-mile ride down the Laredo road and pick us out a place to relieve mister Laredo marshal of Sam Bass."

We got out of town next morning not too long after dawn. I had decided not to get word to Chauncey what we planned. The reason I didn't want to was because I didn't know what a lame-brain like him was liable to do. For all I understood about the boy he was liable to brag to his jailers that his partner was going to free him. Anyway, it wasn't important that he know. The play would be entirely in our hands, and his knowing wouldn't help or hurt.

I figured somewhere around ten miles out of town would get us far away enough from San Antonio while still making it not too long of a ride back. Not that we were going back to San Antonio, at least not me and Chauncey. Naturally we'd have to hide out until time for the robbery.

My plan did not call for Chulo to be an actual part of the holdup of the Laredo marshal. He would wait in San Antonio, watching the jail, and make sure that the marshal did not choose to go overland or take some other route. If he did Chulo was to ride and tell me. But if he took the Laredo road, as I figured he would, Chulo was to stay in San Antonio. Even after I freed Chauncey there would be three nights before the train left, and I wanted Chulo to keep an eye on it. Meanwhile Chauncey and I would hide out somewhere in the rough country near the city.

The four days passed slowly. There wasn't anything to do but lay around town and then go see Cata at night. She had now become, openly, very sweet and loving, though it was not something she talked about. She had even begun to bring me little treats. She brought me some brown sugar candy that she'd made and then a silk bandana that she'd embroidered herself. I put that away because it was too good to use for every day.

She was still very shy and modest about her body. I had had the hardest time getting her to be naked while we were making love, and she still, when we were finished, insisted on pulling the sheet up over her body. One night I pulled the sheet off her over her protests and lay by her side looking at her body in the dim light of the moon shining through the casement window. She did not look near as plump naked as she did with clothes on. Her legs were long and slender, and her waist was no bigger than it had to be. Even her upper body, where Mexican women traditionally get heavy, was not too large. She had excellent breasts, and her face was not uncomely, though it was not beautiful.

One night, laying just like that, I began to talk to her in English, which she didn't understand a word of.

"I wonder," I said aloud, "why I just don't settle on what I can have and quit running around like a blind calf chasing a dream that I'll probably never get anyway."

I was leaning on an elbow, looking down at her. She was laying with her eyes shut tightly and her hands clenched into fists by her side out of embarrassment at laying there naked. But as I talked she opened her eyes and looked up at me, wondering what I was saying.

I smiled at her. "No," I said, still in English, "I'm not going to tell you what I'm saying. I'm just laying here wondering out loud to myself why I don't settle for a good woman like you instead of trying to get something that's way out of my class. Been doing it for better than two years, too, and, if anything, I'm farther away than when I started."

She frowned at me, puzzled, but I went on. "Why don't I take you? You're as good a woman as a man could want. You're pretty, you're very pleasurable to fuck. You'll do anything I tell you. You even act like you love me. You'd cook my meals, wash my clothes, follow me anywhere I wanted to go. And probably never complain. I ought to get that train robbed, take the money, gather you up, and buy a little rancho down in Mexico and set up housekeeping like a normal human being. But here I go, still chasing that girl that I'm beginning to think exists only in my mind. I'm a damn fool, aren't I? Aren't I, Cata?"

Maybe it was the tone of my voice, or maybe it was me using her name which I almost never did. But she put her hand on my arm and looked up into my eyes.

"You're a good woman, Cata," I said. I leaned down and kissed her on the lips. "I don't know what makes me so damn foolish. I don't know why I've always got to be running after something I can't have instead of taking the good things I can have and enjoying them. Like you." I kissed her again, very gently.

Then I rolled off the bed and walked to the washstand by the far wall. There was a lantern there and I lit it. The room bloomed up out of the dim, all whitewashed and puncheon floor. Behind me I heard the sound of the sheet being pulled up as Cata covered herself. There was a mirror on the wall in front of me, and I looked at my face there. It was still boyish looking, but thirty had come and gone. Maybe the boyishness would remain a little longer, but it was getting a little late for the dreams.

I touched a scar on my arm. That had been the first gunshot wound I'd ever sustained. There was another in my thigh, and there was a ragged scar across my chest where the drunk cowboy had surprised me with a knife in the saloon in Atascosa.

But these were just external scars and didn't hurt. I had a few others that couldn't be seen.

Well, I thought, I'd give out more scars than I'd got. And most of the scars I'd give out had been taken to the grave by the gentlemen bearing them.

But I knew one thing, I knew I could honestly say I had never planned to kill nobody. Every man I'd killed had left me no selection but to kill him before he killed me. Now you might say that if a man went for his gun while I was in the commission of robbing him that I was the one done the provoking. Well, that might be right, but then again it don't have to be. I never hurt nobody in a robbery that wasn't a threat to me, but a man's got to realize that if he pulls a gun on me I'm going to kill him. If I can.

Oh, I've killed plenty outside of robberies. Howland Thomas was always trying to get me in fights. He was very quick, in a saloon, to say, "This here's Mr. Wilson Young, 'n if you ain't careful he'll put a hole in you won't hold water." I finally made him cut that nonsense out, but it took a threat to get his attention. Of course, that was Howland, who I consider cost me my two partners. Him and that bank job at Uvalde. Well, I finally killed Howland. Killed him when he was trying to run out on me and Les and Tod after we'd forted up because we couldn't run no farther.

Killed that *hombre* in Arkansas over a woman. His woman by rights. But he'd pushed me into a corner, and I hadn't had no selection. The only reason that one stands out in my mind was because I'd done jail time over it. Not much, but a little jail time is all I want. And I didn't know if I'd killed the deputy sheriff I'd shot when I made my break. I'd never gone back to see.

I didn't know how many it was I'd killed. I didn't want to think about it, tried not to think about it.

I washed my face in a bowl, dried it, and turned back to Cata. She was watching me. I went to the bed, knelt by her, and leaned over and kissed her. She still wouldn't take money. That had bothered me to the point I'd almost decided not to come to her anymore, but I'd thought better of it. And she'd been right. I now felt more comfortable with her, more tender. I guess she'd done it a-purpose and known what she was doing.

"I got to go," I said to her in English.

"*¿Se marcha?*" she asked me.

"*Sí*," I answered. I kissed her again, and she slipped both arms around my neck. Her skin was smooth and cool. "You're a good woman," I said to her again. "Maybe I'll get smart and take you to Mexico with me."

At the word Mexico she looked at me and asked, "*¿Viaja por Mexico?*" I laughed "Someday," I said. "If I get lucky."

The day before they were to leave, the law sent to the hotel for Chauncey's gear. I wasn't there, but the room clerk told me about it. I checked the livery stable, and the man there said he had orders to have Chauncey's horse saddled and ready the next morning at six o'clock.

That confirmed what the cousin had told me.

Chulo and I made out plans that night. His attitude was that his job was too easy, but I assured him how important it was that he keep a watch on that money car, that we had to have one man in town.

I went to bed early that night, bypassing Cata. I was going to have to get up early the next morning to be well in position when Chauncey and the marshal got there.

I rode out about 4 A.M., giving myself plenty of time. In my saddlebags I had gear and food enough to last me and Chauncey the few days until time for the robbery. Me and Chulo had scouted a good hiding place about four miles east of San Antonio on the Salado Creek. My plan was to hold the marshal up, take his

horse and clothes and boots and set him adrift
a good four or five miles from the road with his
hands tied and his feet hobbled. I figured that
would hold him up at least a day. And then
they weren't going to look for us around San
Antonio. Their figuring would be that we'd of
headed south. I didn't figure I had too much to
worry about breaking Chauncey free. It was just
going to mean some dull time hanging around a
hideout.

It was good light when I got to the place I'd
selected for the ambush. There was a cut or a
gully at right angles to the road with a bunch of
boulders and underbrush that kind of screened
the entrance from view. All I planned to do was
let them get abreast of me, then ride out and
throw down on the marshal.

I guessed it to be a little after five so I
pulled into the gully, stepped down, loosened
my horse's cinches, lit a cigarette, and settled
down to wait. After a while the sun got up and
it commenced to get hot. There's very little
spring in that part of Texas, maybe a month
to six weeks. First thing you know it's done
got hot. Of course, not as bad as the border
country where they have two seasons, summer
and August. You don't want to be in the border
country in August.

I smoked and waited, figuring they'd be along
about seven o'clock. I'd brought some cold biscuits from the hotel, and I ate a couple of those
and washed them down with water out of my
canteen.

The waiting was tedium, but it got to finally be what I reckoned by the sun as half-past six, and I put out my cigarette and cinched up my horse. Then I mounted up and rode to the mouth of the gully. I was still screened mostly by the brush so that they wouldn't see me until they were right abreast.

The sun was getting hotter, but I sat motionless while my horse stamped a foot in impatience and switched flies. After a time I heard a clink and the sound of saddle leather creaking. I eased my revolver out of the holster and checked the loading. After a minute more I heard the sound of a voice becoming more distinct. I recognized it as Chauncey's. I couldn't quite make out what he was saying, but he was talking in that high, querulous voice of his so that I knew he was complaining to someone.

Then they came around a bend in the road, and I could see them. The marshal didn't have Chauncey tied or handcuffed, but he had a lariat rope made fast around Chauncey's waist with the other end tied to his saddle horn.

The marshal was just a skinny, ordinary looking *hombre*. He had a rifle in his saddle boot and a revolver on his right hip. He didn't appear to be listening to Chauncey. As they neared I was able to pick up fragments of what Chauncey was complaining about. " . . . no right to take me back to . . . ain't your jurisdiction an' . . ." I imagined he'd been carrying on like that ever since they'd left San Antonio.

I kind of gathered myself up inside and got ready as I drew my revolver and cocked it. And then they were coming by the gully and I rode out.

"Hold it!" I said loudly, leveling my piece at the marshal. Chauncey was a little ahead and on the inside between me and the marshal. They froze instinctively, the marshal actually reining up before Chauncey. For a second he didn't move his head, then he turned slowly to face me.

"Just hold it," I said again, keeping my pistol steady on the marshal's chest. It was beginning to look as if it were going to go as easy as I'd planned.

Then it happened. Chauncey come out of his surprise or his daze or whatever he was in, and his face lit up and he yelled, "Will!" like I was dropping by at Christmas. Then, I'll be goddamned if the fool didn't turn his horse and start to ride toward me. The leash he was on wouldn't let him go far, but he came far enough to get between me and the marshal.

"No! Back!" I yelled at him, but it was too late. He was already in between me and the marshal. I cut my horse to the left, but the marshal was already firing. I felt a deep, burning pain pluck at my side, thinking, in the same instant, that I couldn't have been hit bad else I'd of been knocked out of the saddle. I thumbed off two quick shots, both of them taking the lawman in the chest. I had a clear view of

the surprised look on his face as he flipped
backward off his horse.

It was suddenly very quiet after the boom-
ing of guns. Chauncey sat his horse, his jaw
slack. I didn't say a word to him. Instead I
slid gently out of the saddle and went over
to look at the marshal. He was lying on his
back in the dusty, rocky road. One bullet had
taken him in the throat latch, the other had
hit him in the breastbone. He was plenty dead
all right. I felt bad about it. I hadn't meant to
kill him.

Chauncey rode up beside me and looked
goggle-eyed down at the marshal. "Golly, Will,
you've done killed him."

My side was hurting like hell, and I wanted
to have a look at it. I turned savagely on
Chauncey. "Shut your fucking face, you fool!"
I said. "And get down off that horse!"

I knew something had to be done about the
marshal and in a hurry. Somebody could come
riding along the road at any time. Chauncey
was off his horse now, and I told him to load
the marshal's body on his horse. I think it was
finally coming to him what a fool idiot thing
he'd done getting in between me and the lawman for he got right to work without saying
anything. But he couldn't handle the limp body
without some help, so I took one side and he the
other and we layed the marshal's body cross-
wise over the saddle. Then we taken the lariat
and kind of bound him on so he wouldn't slide
off. I had trouble helping because of my side. I

tried not to think about it. I was afraid to see how badly I was hit.

We finally got him lashed on, and I picked up the lawman's hat and revolver and stuffed them in his saddlebags. "Now get on your horse," I told Chauncey, "and take him way on back out yonder." I waved my hand to indicate the rough country off the road. "Go at least two miles and find a good place to hide him. Hide the body and put all his gear in with him. Don't take nothing. Unsaddle his horse and unbridle him and hide that with the body. Then turn the horse loose." I was talking slowly and carefully, talking to him like a child you had to make understand. "This is important Chauncey. We don't want him found until after the robbery. It would stir the country up and us with a job to pull. So hide him good." I was holding my side with my left hand. I sneaked a look down and saw that my shirt was soaked and my hand bloody. Chauncey looked also and said, judiciously, "That don't look so good, Will. You ought to see to it."

"I will," I said, my anger coming up, "when you get your corn-bread ass moving and get the job done. Now git!"

He looked sullen at my tone, but he mounted and took the marshal's horse on lead and rode into the brush.

"At least a mile or two!" I called after him.

When he was out of sight I led my horse over to the side of the road and took off my shirt. There was a bullet hole in my left side. Bending around I could see where it had exited, leaving a much bigger, ragged hole. That was the way one of them big caliber soft-nosed bullets did; made a little neat hole going in but carried a bunch of meat out with it.

Well, it wasn't too bad. It had passed through muscle and hadn't hit anything else, but the numbness you get when you're first hit was wearing off, and I could feel my side beginning to stiffen up. The first thing to do was keep it from getting infected.

I went over to my saddlebag and got out a bottle of whiskey and a clean shirt. First thing I did was lay on my back and pour whiskey in the hole, hoping it would go all the way through. It burned so bad I could hardly get my breath. I poured more in, clenching my teeth against the pain. I thought I was going to cry out, and tears came to my eyes.

When I could I sat up and tore the shirt into strips. I had to rig something up to make the wound drain. Doctors called it tents. What you had to do with a wound like this was keep it from healing up on the outside and letting the infection get away from you on the inside.

I cut a thin little stick off a mesquite tree with my pocketknife and then skinned it and whittled it down to where it was about the big around of a pencil. Then I soaked one of the strips off my shirt in the whiskey, took a deep breath, and began working the strip into the hole. By the time I got it in there good I was perspiring and shaking. Then I took another strip and worked it in to the other hole, the back one. That was worse because the flesh was so much more torn up. When I was finished I was light-headed and dizzy and felt like I was going to pass out.

After a time I was able to get up. I put my shirt back on, grimacing at the pain, and walked out in the road and looked around. There was no sign of the killing except a dark brown stain in the dust. I stirred it around with my boot and it disappeared. I lit a cigarette and looked off in the direction Chauncey had disappeared. He shouldn't, I reckoned, be back for at least an hour. Meanwhile I ought to get off the road. If somebody came by it would look suspicious me just lollygagging on the side of the road. I led my horse back into the gully and tethered him and then lit a cigarette. My side had stiffened up so that any kind of movement was very painful. But I knew that it would only be worse if I didn't move it as much as possible. Besides, the movement would make it bleed more and help clean it out.

That goddamn Chauncey, I thought. That dumb, piss-headed, fuck head. I didn't know what to do about him, what to say to him. I ought to take my pistol and whip the shit out of him, I thought. But I knew it wouldn't do any good. He probably didn't even know he'd done anything wrong. Everything he did he did like a fool a-fuckin'—without fear or forethought.

No, I thought, there wasn't much point in saying or doing anything to him. It would just be a waste. Best thing was to just get through the job and split up as soon as possible.

That is if he didn't get me killed on the job.

He came back sooner than I'd expected. I rode out to meet him as he came up on the road. Before I could say a word he said, "Listen, I want you to know I'm grateful for you springing me from the law. But I been thinkin', and I want it clear I don't consider that to give you the right to talk to me like you did. I ain't no goddamn child and I—"

I cut him off, looking at him wonderingly. "I got a bad feeling," I said, "that you ain't got sense enough to know what you did."

"See? There you go again. And blamin' me for something that wadn't my fault. Gettin' arrested. What if it had been you that had got arrested? I bet it would just have been a accident, then. But—"

He didn't know what he'd done. I looked at him like you would a bug. "It ain't you getting arrested," I said mildly. "It's because you're a dangerous fool, Chauncey."

"Now wait a minute. Listen—"

"You're a fool," I said evenly. "You did a fool thing, but you are such a fool you don't even know what you did." My voice was getting softer. "You got in between me and a man I had covered, Chauncey," I said. "You got me shot, Chauncey. You almost got me killed."

He was looking at me blankly, but it was starting to come home to him.

"But that's the last time, Chauncey," I said, my voice as soft as ever. "I'm going to go ahead with this job, but after that I'm going to shuck your corn-bread ass. But I'm not going to let you get me or Chulo killed. If you do any more foolish, dangerous things I'm going to kill you. Do you understand, Chauncey? I'm going to shoot you and kill you. Immediately you do something. Now do you hear me?"

He wiped a hand nervously across his face. "Hell, Will . . ." he said, "I mean I never thought about gettin' in between you and that—I mean . . ."

"That's right," I said, "you never thought. Well, the next time you don't think it'll be your last time."

I cinched my horse up. He slowly remounted. "Did you hide that lawman good?"

"Pretty well," he said. The fear was still on his face. It was beginning to sink in that it was his action that had caused me to get hit. He swallowed. "Uh, how's your side?"

I looked at him for a long moment without answering. Then I said, "Let's go."

We rode almost to San Antonio then circled around to the west, striking Salado Creek and turning up it for a mile or so. I'd found a hideout about a quarter of a mile from the creek back in a little oak thicket. Not that we had to be that careful. Chauncey could camp here just like any traveler. Unless a lawman who knew he was supposed to be in jail came by, there was no danger.

He had his sleeping gear, and I'd brought a skillet and some grub. There was plenty of water in the creek and plenty of grazing for his horse. Anyway, it wouldn't be for but a couple of days.

We got down, and Chauncey loose cinched his horse and put him on a picket rope. He still didn't know that I didn't plan to stay there. Hell, there was no reason for me to crouch out in the bushes like some goddamn Indian. I could go into town now, now that the lawman was dead and there was no one to raise the alarm about me freeing Chauncey.

But Chauncey hadn't caught onto that yet. I helped him arrange the camp then untied my horse and mounted. He looked up at me. "Where you going?"

"Into town," I said. "Chulo and I will be back out in two nights."

"What? Hey, what the hell! You're not going to leave me out here by myself!"

"Yes I am." I leaned slightly out of the saddle. "And Chauncey—Don't come into town. Don't leave this camp."

"But Will—"

"Remember what I told you, Chauncey," I said. "I meant it. You leave this camp and you better keep on running." Then I wheeled my horse and rode away without looking back.

Chulo didn't seem overly disturbed about my having to kill the marshal. "There are risks in the line of work," was all he said, but he didn't say whether he thought it was me or the lawman doing the risk-taking.

Having given up my hotel room I stayed at

the cousin's house, just going ahead and openly
bunking in with Cata. The next afternoon me
and Chulo rode out to look at the place where
we were going to board the money car. It was
about two miles out of town, in the middle of
a big curve the track took to go around a considerable hill. There was a tool shack or shed
cut into the side of the hill and shoved right
up next to the track. I guess it was up close so
they could load and unload tools out of boxcars
without no great deal of trouble. Anyway, it
was ideal for our designs. We could come down
the hill and get on top of the shed, which was
plenty tall, and be all set to jump on the money
car as it came past. And the train would be
going awful slow while it made its way around
the curve. That part of it looked like a cinch.
We'd start about midnight the night before by
riding over to the shack. Then me and Chulo
would hide out on the hill until just before the
train came while Chauncey lit out with the
horses for the water station.

That meant, of course, that we were not going
to be able to see the gold loaded. And that was
the part that worried me the most. Chauncey
said they brought it over to the money car
from the bank just before daybreak. Said they
brought it over in a padlocked strongbox that
we could open with a crowbar or just shoot off. ·

Well, all I could say was that we had no
choice but to believe him. I hoped he knew
what he was talking about for his own sake.

Because, if he didn't, I wouldn't have to worry about killing him. Chulo would.

On the afternoon of the night we was leaving I was sitting out on the cousin's patio reading a book. I was reading a book by Sir Walter Scott called *Ivanhoe*. I'd been carrying it around in my saddlebags for better than a month, but, what with one thing and another, I seldom got a chance to read it, and reading was a thing I'd been partial to ever since I was a boy. This Ivanhoe was a knight back in olden England times. I'd been taken by the way he was searching and hunting, just like myself. Those *hombres* in those days really put women up on a pedestal, acting like they'd break if you treated them like ordinary people. That made me squirm a little when I'd first read about it because it sort of reminded me of what I was doing with that Linda girl. But thinking on it I decided that wasn't the case. I mean, I wanted to marry this girl and get the advantage of being related to quality and having a high-class wife. And I wasn't going to put her on no pedestal either. I didn't think of her like I did a lot of other women, but I planned on enjoying her.

The sun was nice and warm, and I put the book down and let myself speculate on Linda for just a bit. I had the good feeling that this job was going to go all right, in spite of the things that seemed to be against it. And if it came off, and if I got back across the border with my cut of the money, I'd be in pretty good condition to press my suit. That gave me a little excited feeling inside. I felt like I was closer to my goal than anytime since I'd seen the girl.

About that time Cata came out to me. She'd brought me a glass of lemonade along with a bottle of tequila. There was a little wooden table by the chair I was sitting in, and she put it on top of that and then stood there, her hands together in front of her, looking down at me.

"Why thanks, Cata," I said. I took a drink of the tequila, right out of the bottle, then chased it with lemonade. "Aaah," I said, "that's damn good." The tequila burned going down, but then it hit bottom and began to spread out. The lemonade was cool and tart. It went very well with the tequila.

There was another chair, but Cata didn't sit down. And she wouldn't until I asked her to. I finally did, watching her as she sat down, watching the way she kept her hands folded in her lap.

We didn't talk. She just sat there while I drank tequila and lemonade. It was comfortable sitting with her and not talking. Thinking about it I realized I had felt comfortable around her from almost the very first. But I looked at her, wondering what she was thinking, wondering if she was thinking about me and what I was.

She may have known about my profession, but it wasn't because I'd told her. Thinking back I realized I'd never told her much of anything about myself. I doubted if she knew, sitting there looking calm, that I was leaving this night, leaving to go rob a train. Of course I knew she didn't know about the train. The cousin didn't even know about that.

"Well, Cata," I said, catching her eyes, "I'll be taking off tonight, and I don't reckon I'll ever see you again."

She looked calmly back at me, not understanding the English, not even asking me in Spanish what I'd said.

"Yeah," I went on, "we're going to rob a train. I'll come out with my share being around twelve, thirteen thousand. I'm gonna take that and head for Mexico and marry me the daughter of a rich don and raise horses. What do you think of that for a plan?"

A little wrinkle appeared between her eyes as she strained to catch any word of Spanish that might help her understand.

I got tired of the game. "Hell with," I said, and laughed. She smiled at my laughter. I took another drink of the whiskey and got up. I decided I might as well have her one last time. I'd be laying out in the bush for two weeks, and I'd got used to having a woman since I'd been in San Antonio. I went up to her and lifted her face by the chin and leaned down and kissed her. Her arms went immediately around my neck. I could feel her soft breasts pressing up against me. My breathing started to pick up.

"Let's go," I said to her huskily in Spanish. "To the room."

She got up without a word and led me by the hand into the house and down the hall to the room we slept in.

It was dim in the room, but she still undressed in the corner with her back to me, doing it quickly and shyly and then jumping into bed and pulling up the sheet. I undressed more slowly, taking my time because my side was so stiff. She lay there watching me. That was what I couldn't understand. She was shy about being naked but she always liked to watch me. I climbed into bed and was going to lay down beside her, but she raised up to examine my side. I'd wrapped a long bandage around my waist, a piece of bed linen, and she wanted me to take it off so she could see how it was doing. I shook my head, no. I didn't want to be bothered. Desire was already in me and I wanted what we'd come to the room for.

But she kept insisting, so I finally unwrapped the bandage and let her look. It looked all right to me. There was some redness around the two wounds, but it looked like it was draining pretty good. The tents were still hanging out of each of the two holes. I made myself a mental thought that I was going to have to change them before the night was out. I didn't look forward to it for I knew the wounds were a good deal sorer than they were when I put them in right after the shooting.

Cata put her soft, cool hands on the skin of my side, feeling to see if there was any fever there. The first night I was back she'd made a big to-do about it, looking horrified and shaking her head. It was her who'd got me the strips of bed linen to bandage it. One good thing in her favor—she hadn't asked me how it happened, though I knew she could clearly see it was a gunshot wound. But, then, I guess when you're married to a cattle thief and have a brother who deals in stolen horses and cattle, you learn not to ask too many questions.

I hadn't been worried about the wound, but I was glad it was doing as well as it had. Other than the stiffness, which was pretty painful sometimes, it hadn't bothered me too bad. I felt a little worried that I hadn't changed the tents and poured some more whiskey in it, but I guess I hadn't because of the bother and the pain.

There was something in our lovemaking that afternoon that I didn't quite know what to make of. My desire somehow turned into something softer, something like tenderness. I guess she felt it in me for it made her act more like she'd been acting. It gave me a kind of uncomfortable feeling, like I was making love to her the last time and not ever expecting to see her again.

Which was what I was expecting. The thing that worried me about the way I was feeling was why I should care if I never saw her again. She was nothing to me. I had my plans made. She didn't figure in any of them. And, yet, there I was being tender and feeling all lovey or something.

I was still even feeling it when we got ready to leave the room. I stopped her at the door and took both her hands in mine and looked down into her face. "Cata," I said, "look, I'm going to have to go and I probably won't be back. But you been damn good to me. Real good. You're a good woman and I wish that you think of me from time to time. I know I'll think of you."

Her face flinched when I said that about maybe never seeing her again, but, other than that, she made no sign.

I went ahead and kissed her and left the room to go hunt up Chulo. It was about time for us to make our way out to Chauncey's camp.

It was just after dark when we rode into Chauncey's camp. The thick growth of trees kept the remains of his supper fire hid from us until we were right up on it. He got up, dusting off the seat of his britches, as we dismounted. I nodded and Chulo said, "Hallo, *niño*."

I didn't know if Chauncey had left camp or not. I hadn't been out to see. But it didn't much matter now because we'd be pulling out in another hour or two. I got a bottle of whiskey out of my saddlebags and we all hunkered around the fire and passed the bottle around. Both Chulo's and my saddlebags were loaded with provisions we'd bought to use at our hideout after the robbery to add on to what we'd already cached there.

"Well, *salud!*" I said, raising the bottle in a toast and then drinking. I passed it along to Chulo.

"*Buena suerte*," he said.

"Yeah, good luck," Chauncey said, taking the bottle from the black Mexican.

"Getting pretty close," I said. "Hope we haven't forgotten anything."

I couldn't think of anything. We had the robbery planned, the hideout taken care of, the route we'd take to Mexico. That seemed about it. All we had to worry about was that gold being on the train, and there wasn't a damn thing we could do about that except trust Chauncey. I eyed him for a moment. "Get tired of staying out here, Chaunce?"

He looked back, a little of the sullenness in his eyes, "I been in places I'd ruther be."

"But you stuck it out?"

"Yes, I stuck it out!" he said, flaring. "I didn't leave the goddamn camp."

Chulo spoke up, his dry voice cutting through the dark night. "But of course he has given you much thanks for making him free from the lawman who was transporting him to Laredo, no?"

"Oh, yes," I said, grinning slightly. "He thanked me all right. Ol' Chauncey is a boy knows his manners. Can't never fault him that department."

Chulo made a little snort. He knew the story of the gunshot wound I'd sustained in my side, though I'd painted it some better for fear he'd get totally disgusted with Chauncey and pull out.

Chauncey didn't say anything, just turned his head and glowered into the fire.

"Give me that bottle," I said to Chulo. "Going to be a long night." I took a pull, watching the two of them over the bottle. If the gold was there it was going to be all right. If it wasn't, me and Chulo would get a nice long train ride for nothing.

"Well," I said after a little more time had passed, "best we get moving. You got a long ride tonight Chauncey, and me and Chulo has got the side of a mountain to try and sleep on."

We got to the tool shed, the place we were going to board the train, at what I calculated to be a little after midnight. Chulo and I dismounted, slipped the bits out of our horses' mouths, put them on a lead rope, and turned them over to Chauncey. I stood by his saddle looking up at his young face. "All right, Chaunce," I said, "we'll see you tomorrow morning. Be sure and have everything under control."

"I'll handle that, goddamnit," he said, "you just hold up your end."

He rode away into the darkness leading our two horses. Chulo and I had only our revolvers, along with plenty of extra cartridges, and some bread and meat. We'd seen no reason to bring our rifles, not for the close work we were anticipating.

"Well," I said, "let's get at it." The outline of the hill lay above us in the night sky, and we began laboriously climbing up its steep side. Off to my left I could see the lights of San Antonio. But where we were all was quiet, the shack and the tracks the only evidence that we were near civilization.

We climbed upward for two or three hundred yards. Climbed until we'd found a good clump of cedar to hide in. Then we settled in and made a little supper out of bread and meat. Chulo produced a welcome bottle of whiskey he'd had in his short coat.

"Well," I said. "Ain't nothing to do now except wait. And hope the train's on time."

"And the gold is there," Chulo added softly.

"And the gold is there," I agreed.

CHAPTER 6

The sun had been up a good hour when we made our way down the hill and onto the roof of the shed, laying flat so we wouldn't be seen. Not that it seemed necessary. The area was deserted as far as we could see. We lay there feeling the sun getting hotter and hotter on our backs. The shack had a tin roof and would get plenty hot if the sun got much higher. I had a wad of oily rags stuffed down in my shirt. Chulo had raised his eyebrows at them, but hadn't asked what they were for. He'd know soon enough.

We lay without speaking, looking back up toward town for the first sign of the train. Overhead a few vultures wheeled slowly through the clear sky. I asked Chulo for the third time if he had the hacksaw.

"*Sí*," he said.

I said, "I hope we don't have to kill the clerk in the baggage car." Then added, "And I hope he's alone. I just hope to hell there ain't no shooting."

"Sometimes," Chulo said philosophically,

"such matters are impossible to avoid."

Which was something that didn't require no answer. As I damn well knew.

Then we heard the first thin chuff chuff chuff of the train. I heard it first, and I said, "Here it comes."

We saw it coming through between two hills about a mile and a half off.

"You'll jump first," I told Chulo, "and I'll be right behind you. Ain't no way to do it, but try and land as soft as you can."

I began to tense up as the train got nearer and nearer. I guess there are *hombres* who can go in on a job without getting all wired up, but I'm not one of them. There may have been a time, in my younger days, when I was hell for leather and let the devil take the hindmost, but those days were past. I guess when a man gets to be thirty he begins to calculate the risks a little closer. I was willing to take the risks for the gain involved, but that didn't mean I looked forward to them.

And then the train was there. It came to us around the curve going very slowly, maybe five miles an hour. It was a passenger train with four coaches, then a mail car, and then the money car with a caboose on at the end.

We let the engine pass and then two of the coaches before we raised up. The top of the cars were just right there. Maybe a foot below us and about three feet away. Getting on was going to be easy.

"That's it," I said to Chulo, "coming up." My

throat was tight when I tried to speak.

The money car got opposite us, and Chulo jumped, landing on all fours. He'd lit about midway down the car. I followed him, having no trouble landing on the car. It was swaying slightly, but not enough to give me trouble about balance.

Without a word we worked our way back to the lid over the ventilation hole. As near as I could make out, the padlock was the same as I'd seen that night in the freight yard.

We hunkered around the lid, which was kind of like a big, flat box.

"Give me the hacksaw," I said to Chulo, "then keep an eye fore and aft. Don't let nobody walk up on us."

Not that there was much chance of that, being highly unlikely that anyone could have seen us make the jump.

I took the hacksaw and started in sawing on the ring of the padlock. It was worse than I'd expected, being hard-tempered steel. I was plenty glad that we'd brought several extra blades. I could see that we were going to need them.

Once around the curve the train had begun to pick up speed and the swaying had increased. I sawed for about half an hour then turned it over to Chulo. The saw had cramped my hand, and I had to flex it several times to get the stiffness out of it.

"*Mucho duro*," Chulo said, puffing a little.

"Yeah," I agreed. The ring was about half an

inch thick, and we'd cut about midway through it.

After a while we changed blades, and I spelled Chulo for a time. It was slow going, but little by little the cut was increasing. We worked silently. Now that the train was going fast, the wind made it hard to hear.

Finally the cut was all the way through. I looked at Chulo and blew out my breath. My hand was cramping and sore.

Next I took my pistol barrel and stuck it in the ring of the lock and pried the two jaws apart that the cut had made. It was no way to be treating a fine shooting revolver, but it didn't seem to hurt it none. I took the padlock off and looked at Chulo. He grimaced slightly. I didn't think he was looking forward to dropping blind into the railroad car anymore than I was. We could only hope that anyone that was inside hadn't heard the noise of our work.

I rested a minute, looking around. I calculated we were some twenty miles out of San Antonio. It was near time to get on with it.

I took the oil rags out of my shirt. I'd picked them up at a blacksmith shop in San Antonio. Then I turned my back to the wind and got out one of those big, yellow-headed phosphorous matches. I had a whole pocketful of them, having anticipated that I'd have trouble lighting the rags in the wind. After several tries I got one going, and I held it and the rest of them up in the wind until they all caught and started smoldering, putting out a lot of thick, black smoke that rose to join the stream from the smokestack of the train engine.

I looked at Chulo and motioned toward the vent top. He nodded and took it in both hands and jerked it off, and I threw the bundle of smoldering rags into the opening, and Chulo immediately popped the top back on.

We sat back and looked at each other. I guess we waited about five minutes, and then I lifted the vent top. A gust of smoke came boiling out.

"It's working," I said. I put the lid back on for a moment or two more.

Chulo said, "How many?"

"I don't know," I said. It was impossible to hear any noise from within because of the rush of the wind and the sound of the train. I lifted the lid again and, turning my head against the smoke, listened in the car.

"Can't tell," I said to Chulo. "I hear coughing but I can't tell if it's just one man or more."

Now I left the lid off, letting the smoke stream out. I looked at Chulo. "Ready?"

My plan was simply to jump in before all the smoke got out, be drawn and ready when it cleared up, and have the drop on anybody inside. I said to Chulo, "I'd bet there's not but one man in there."

He made a half-smile. "Very gracious of you to bet our ass."

"Let's do it," I said. I shoved my revolver into my belt and then swung my legs into the hole and, holding onto both sides, slowly let myself down into the car. Hanging, I felt with

my feet as far as I could reach. All I felt was
space. I let myself drop. I landed softly, letting my knees flex, holding my breath against
the smoke. It was still very thick and I could
see nothing, but I could hear someone coughing. I immediately moved to one side for I was
crouched where Chulo must land. In another
half-second I heard him land beside me. I put
out a hand, touching his shoulder. He flinched,
but remained still. My eyes were burning and
watering, but the smoke was escaping very rap-
idly through the open ventilation hole. I got my
revolver in my right hand and cocked it, hearing Chulo do the same an instant behind mine.
And now the smoke was really clearing and
we could almost see. We crouched, our guns
outstretched, ready to fire at an instant. There
was only one man. He was leaned up against
the sliding side door, clawing at his face, trying to get a breath of air from a crack in the
door. I didn't think he was even aware of our
presence. I looked at Chulo and let myself grin
just a little.

The rags were laying in the middle of the
floor, still smoldering and putting out considerable smoke. I got up and began to stomp them
out. At the sound the man turned with a great
big surprised look on his face. I pointed my pistol at him. "Just take it easy, *hombre*," I said.

He was a clerk-looking kind of fellow. Behind
his glasses his eyes got as big as doorknobs. He
opened his mouth once or twice but didn't say
anything.

I finished stomping the rags out then scooped them up and pitched them out the opening in the roof. Chulo came up beside me. The clerk was frozen with his hands in the air.

"Well, here we are," I said.

"*Sí*," Chulo said and nodded.

I was suddenly very thirsty. I looked at the terrified clerk. "You got any water?"

He stared back at me, a blank look on his face.

"Water," I waved my gun impatiently at him. "You got any water? To drink? Water to drink?"

He acted like he was paralyzed, but he kind of half-pointed toward the corner where a little desk was. "In the jug," he croaked. "Water."

I went over and got the jug while Chulo watched him. I don't know why my mouth always got dry on a job, but it did. I guess it was a common thing because I've seen *hombres* spit to prove they weren't scared, something I could never do.

I took a deep pull on the water and then offered it to Chulo. He shook his head so I corked it and put it back on the clerk's desk. A railroader's watch was laying on the top, and I taken note that it was a little after nine o'clock. The train generally hit the water station, according to Chauncey, at about eleven, so we had plenty of time. So far the job was going as well as I wanted.

I turned my attention to the clerk. "What's your name?"

"Ha-Ha-Hawkins," he stuttered.

"No, your first name. Your calling name."

"Tom," he said.

"All right, Tom," I said, "put your hands down. You ain't got nothing to be scairt of so long as you don't give us no trouble."

It took him a moment, but he finally put his hands down. He still looked might uneasy.

"We're here for the gold."

He didn't say anything.

"I said we're here for the gold. Where's it at?"

He shook his head slowly. "Ain't no gold. Not here."

"Now, Tom," I said, "let's don't have any of that kind of talk. Now where's the gold?"

He shook his head again. "Ain't no gold in this car. This here's a mail car, and we don't carry no gold."

I was getting a little sinking feeling in the pit of my stomach. The clerk sounded and looked so sincere. But I said, "Bullshit, Tom, this ain't no mail car. There's no mail sacks in here."

And indeed it did not look like a mail car. All that was in the car was a bunch of boxes stacked along one wall. Then there were some more in a little chicken wire cage in a corner. Other than that and the clerk's desk and a potbellied stove for heat in the winter, there wasn't anything else in the car.

"Well," the clerk said, "it's not exactly a mail car, but it's an express car. For freight and such."

"And gold," I said. "Now look—" I sounded

as threatening as I could, "Now look, we know there's gold coin on here bound for the banks in Laredo. We've come for it, and we plan to take it, and all you'll do is get yourself hurt if you try and stop us. Now where is it!"

He swallowed, looking frightened again. "I— I—I don't know about any gold. Honest to God."

Chulo said in a growl, "Forget him. Let us look ourselves."

"Wait a minute," I said. "We've got plenty of time." I studied the clerk. He sure sounded sincere, which scared the hell out of me. But I noticed the scared glances he'd been shooting over at Chulo. I looked around at the black Mexican. He did look some kind of fierce, especially with that big revolver in his hand.

"Now, look," I said to the clerk. "Look, Tom, I'm a reasonable man myself, and I might not get mad and do anything awful to you if there ain't no gold on here. But that's just me." I let my eyes wander toward Chulo. "My partner here," I said, "he ain't quite so easygoing about such things as not finding gold where he expects it. See, he's put quite a store about finding gold. He needs it. You understand what I'm saying?"

The clerk was now looking at Chulo. I kept expecting him to raise his hands again.

"You understand what I'm saying?"

He nodded kind of jerkily, not taking his eyes off Chulo.

"What I'm trying to tell you," I went on, "is that even though I could take it, I'm not sure the Indian here—" Chulo gave me a look. "I'm not sure the Indian here wouldn't do something kind of awful. You get what I mean? I mean, I can't handle him so I wouldn't be no help. So why don't you go to thinking where that gold is? We're getting short on time."

The clerk swallowed, but didn't say anything.

Chulo begin to make growling sounds and cocked his pistol. "Now look," I said, "that old dog won't hunt, Tom. We *know* you've got gold on board, and you might just as well save us the trouble of hunting it up."

"I don't know anything about any gold," he said, still watching Chulo.

The black Mexican suddenly let loose a string of Mexican oaths. He holstered his gun and took out his big clasp knife and opened it. "By God," he said in English, "I'm going to cut off his fucking nose and ears! Fucking gringo liar!"

The clerk looked like he was getting limp. He put his hands up and backed to the wall as Chulo came up to him, holding the big, glinting knife out in front of him. Chulo looked fierce, all right. If I'd of been the clerk I'd of been plenty scared.

"I don't know about no gold!" the clerk said, his voice rising up at the end.

"No?" Chulo said. He put the point of his knife inside the clerk's right nostril.

"Where gold?" he said.

The clerk was sweating. He swallowed. "Dunno."

All of a sudden Chulo jerked the knife, cutting clean through the clerk's nostril. Bright red blood cascaded down his face and shirt. The knife was so sharp that it took an instant for the pain to hit him and then the clerk screamed. He put his hand to his nose. It came away covered with blood. "Gawd!" he yelled. "You've cut off my goddamn nose!"

"Just a little piece," Chulo said with a grin that looked like a skull's head. He put his knife in the clerk's other nostril. The little man tried to draw back, but his head was stopped by the wall behind him. "Where's the gold?" Chulo asked him again. "And when the nose gone then comes ears. One at a time. Now, where is the gold?"

For a second the clerk thought he wasn't going to answer. I'm sure he figured we were just broadsiding in the dark. That we didn't know about the bank's gold. But when he seen we knew he decided that his nose and ears was too high a price. He said, pointing toward the chicken wire cage with one of his upraised arms, "Over yonder. In a packing box. The one marked to Jeffrey Cattle Co."

"All right, Tom," I said. "You made you a good selection. You'd looked pretty bad runnin' around smooth faced. Now you go on over yonder and sit at your desk and behave yourself."

We went over to the wire cage and jerked the door open and hunted through the packing crates until we found the one marked as the clerk had told us. Naturally it was at the bottom of the pile. I could see how they worked

it now. And it was as safe a way as any—safe
unless you knew what Chauncey knew. First
you had the secrecy. Then you had the goods
disguised so they'd be hard to find. I doubted,
going to work ripping open the packing box, if
we'd of gone through all the crates in that car. I
imagined we would have got discouraged after
ten or twenty of them.

We drug the box out of the cage and started
on it. It was uncommonly heavy and, dragging
it, hurt my side, which had not been bothering
me before. The crate itself was wood. We asked
the clerk for tools, but he said he had none. He
was sitting in his chair holding a waste rag to
his bleeding nose and looking about half-sick.

We looked around and finally found a heavy
iron bar that we used to prize some of the boards
off the side of the crate. We got them off, but
only after much straining, and then the work
went a little easier. But we still couldn't see the
money box. The inside was stuffed with old rags
and newspapers, and we presumed the box was
inside that. Then we finally got enough boards
off so that we could jerk the stuffing material
out of the crate, and there, sure enough, was
the money box. My heart gave a bound.

"That's it, Chulo!" I said.

"*Sí*," he said. For the first time I heard some
enthusiasm in his voice. I knelt and began trying to drag the box out of the crate. It was
heavy and it was awkward, kneeling like I was.
I jerked and jerked and then had to give up
because my side was hurting like sixty. I said,

"You better get it, Chulo, this damn side is bothering me." I put my hand over the wound. Chulo was staring at it.

He said: "You better look to yourself, *hombre*. You're all over blood."

I looked down. My shirt was soaked. "Goddamnit," I swore, "I've tore it loose."

"You better do something."

"In a minute," I said. "I want to see that box."

Chulo worked it out of the crate, and we stood around admiring it. It was all steel and had a padlock on it about the same bigness as the one we'd just cut through on the vent lid.

"I want to see that gold," I said.

"*¿Cómo no?*" Chulo said. "I also. You think we have to cut it?"

"Naw. See if you can shoot it open. But mind you fire straight down. Wouldn't want no ricochets in here."

I crouched down while Chulo fired at the ring of the lock. Nothing much happened so he fired again, hitting the body of the lock on top. It seemed to give a little. He fired again, and then I tried it while he reloaded. Every time we'd shoot, bits of lead would fly off the lock where the bullet hit. One of them hit me in the leg and went through my pants.

Finally we had it almost off. We took the heavy iron bar and whacked it until it gave up. I knelt and jerked off the lock and opened the lid.

"There it is," I said, softly.

It lay in the box, all stacked tightly in rows, wedged in by wood dividers.

"*Chiuahaha!*" Chulo said reverently.

"Yeah. That's a bunch of gold."

From behind us the clerk said, "You better leave that gold alone. That's the bank's gold."

Chulo and I laughed. "Not anymore," I said.

We stood there looking at it for a moment. "We'll put it into some of those canvas sacks over yonder," I said. "It's too heavy to carry in one bunch. We'll divide it into three sacks."

"You better look at your side first," Chulo said.

He was right; it was bleeding so much the top of my britches were soaked.

I took my shirt off. It was bleeding out the front wound only. The tents I'd put in the night before I hadn't pushed in as far as the first ones partly because of the pain and partly because I figured it had already healed up some on the inside. I pulled the tent out and the blood gushed for a second and then slowed. "I need a rag," I said. There were rags in among the newspapers that had surrounded the money box, and I took a wad of those, pressed them up against the wound, and then rewrapped the long bandage around my waist to hold them in place. That would staunch the bleeding, I figured. The rag itself was none too clean, and I was wishing I'd of had some whiskey to pour in it, but I figured the wound was maybe healed up enough to be on past infection. And, what the hell, it looked like our luck was turning up anyway.

We got three sacks and divided the gold up amongst them. My, that was a power of gold. I knew there was at least forty thousand dollars there, maybe more. It was just a pure pleasure to handle it. Me and Chulo kept grinning at each other while we worked. We didn't try to count too carefully, just kind of guessed at it.

The sacks were still heavy. I figured each one weighed at least fifty pounds apiece. We drug them over by the door.

"That's that," I said to Chulo, wiping the sweat off my face. It was plenty hot in the car.

Ol' Tom was still sitting over at his desk sulking at us, holding the rag up to his nose. He really was a bloody mess, though I don't reckon he had much more on him that I did on me. My side was doing all right, but I was still a little worried about it.

"Hell, Tom," I said. "Don't take on so. It ain't like it was your gold."

"No, but I'll be blamed," he said, his voice coming muffled through the rag.

"Oh, what are you talking about," I said. "Just look at you. It'll look like you put up one hell of a fight. What time of day is it getting to be?"

He looked at his watch but wouldn't answer me for a minute. "Tom?" I said, a little menace in my voice.

"Near ten," he said gruffly. Oh, he was pouting and no mistake.

"About an hour and a half to be on the safe side," I told Chulo. "We better see to getting this door opened."

"It's locked," Tom said, a little note in his voice. "Got to be opened from the outside."

"Maybe," I said. I'd already taken note of that fact, but I'd figured we could prize it away with the iron bar we'd found. I knew it was locked with a little dinky padlock on a hasp like regular mail cars were. It was one of them double sliding doors and, pushing it away a little, I could peer through the crack and see that lock, just about six inches away, bouncing and jumping with the motion of the train. I showed it to Chulo.

"We shoot the *chinga* off," he said.

"Let's try prizing it first."

With Tom watching us we took the bar and wedged it into the door as best we could and strained against it. It wouldn't work because we couldn't get a good enough hold of the door with the end of the bar. It kept slipping off. Otherwise it would have been a piece of cake. Once it felt as if the hasp was pulling loose where it was screwed into the wood of the car, but then the bar slipped, and we fell back.

"Shoot the son of a bitch off," I said in disgust.

Chulo got himself wedged up against the door, right where he could see the lock. He was pushing out the door with his body, but his gun barrel wouldn't quite go through, just the tip enough to give him a clear shot. Hell, the damn lock wasn't a foot away. He was kind of crouched down, his gun up much closer to his face than it ordinarily would have been because of the position he was in and the necessity of aiming. He fired and cursed. "It jumps away," he said. "The *mierda*."

He fired again and suddenly swore and fell back, clapping his hand to his eye.

"What the hell?" I said.

But Chulo was bent over, his hand to his eye, swearing steadily. I finally got him straightened up to where I could see what was wrong. His left eye was a mess, blood was coming out of it, and it was already commencing to swell up so that it was almost shut.

"Goddamn!" I swore. Best I could figure a lead fragment had bounced back off that lock, and bad luck that it was, had somehow come through that little crack and got Chulo in the eye.

"You've had a light put out," I said matter-of-factly.

Chulo was cussing steadily, his face tight against the pain. There wasn't much we could do except get one of the rags, tear it in a long strip, and then bind it around Chulo's head, covering the eye. He'd let up on the swearing a little, but you could see it was killing him.

I didn't say it aloud, but I was thinking to myself that the job was running in awful bad luck. First my side and the Chulo's eye. But a man don't want to go talking about bad luck or else he'll call up more.

There wasn't anything else we could do about Chulo, but there was still the matter of the door. I went ahead and did what I should have done in the first place, shoot the hasp away from the inside, shooting through the wood of the car to where it was easy to figure the hasp was. Three shots and it was gone and I slid the door back. I was plenty disgusted with myself. If I'd been thinking Chulo would never have got hurt, and now, here, it looked like he'd lost an eye.

"And I'm supposed to be running this show," I said disgustedly. "I haven't got sense enough to pour piss out of a boot with the directions on the heel."

"The hell with it," Chulo said. He was a tough son of a bitch and no mistake. *"No importa,"* he said.

"No importa," I said sourly. "Sure, it's just your eye."

"We got the gold," he said.

"Yeah. Yeah." I looked over at the sacks. "Let's hope we get a chance to spend it."

The countryside was rolling past outside the open door. I went to it and leaned out and looked up ahead of the train. We were already starting to hit the flat plains country. I didn't ask Tom what time it was, but went to his desk and looked at his watch. It was crowding eleven.

"Not long now," I said. I went and hunkered down beside Chulo who had his back up against the wall. He had his hand over his eye.

"*Mierda*," he said, "I wish I had a drink of wheesky." He grimaced. I reckoned he was holding himself pretty tight against the pain.

"Not much longer now," I said. "Maybe a half an hour. And we got whiskey in the saddlebags. Plenty of whiskey."

We sat there, rocking with the motion of the train, listening to the rails click. Old Tom wasn't saying anything.

CHAPTER 7

We felt the train slowing, and I jumped up and went to the door. Leaning out I could see the water station about a mile or so ahead. I turned back to Chulo. "Coming up," I said. He got up and joined me at the door, looking out with his one good eye. The side of his face was swole up, and blood and a kind of clear fluid was running down his cheek out from under the bandage. I didn't know what we could do about it. I'd looked in it as best I could through the blood but hadn't been able to see no piece of lead or nothing. But there was no time to think about that now. The water station was coming right up to us. I looked around at Tom, drawing my gun. "Now you jest set still. We're gonna be gone here in a moment and be no more bother to you."

"Look, Will," Chulo said from the doorway. I leaned out with him, expecting to see Chauncey standing there holding the horses. There was Chauncey all right, but he wasn't holding no horses.

"What the hell!" I said. And then we were stopping, and Chauncey was almost in front of us. He was just standing there. And then I noticed he wasn't wearing his gun.

"Oh, shit!" I said. "Something else is wrong!"

Then Chauncey was right in front of the door. We stared at each other for a second. I was in the opening of the door, and Chulo was hid just behind the edge.

"What's up, Chaunce?" I asked. He had a real hangdog look on his face.

"Better get down, Will," he said. "We're done for."

Then I seen the shotgun pointing out the door of the shack, trained on Chauncey's back. I figured it was the old man. But what I seen about that shotgun made me believe it couldn't swing to the left or the right too easily. The crack was too narrow.

I said lowly, to Chulo, "Mark the shotgun at the door."

Chauncey said: "Better get down, Will. You and Chulo. He's a-gonna shoot me if you don't."

Of course at that instant I didn't give a damn if the old man shot him or not. Out of the corner of my mouth I said to Chulo. "Take a quick shot at the door, Chulo. You don't have to hit him. I'll do that."

Chauncey said, sounding a little worried, "Will! Ya'll don't try nothin'. Honest to God, that old man is a-gonna blow me sky high with that scattergun."

That was his lookout. I'd save his ass all I

was going to. And if he couldn't handle a simple job like taking a shack-ass water station from an old man, he deserved to have a hole blowed through him. "Now," I said to Chulo, and he come whipping around the edge and thrumbed off two quick shots at the door. As he did I dropped to one knee and squeezed off two more, aiming carefully, intending to kill whomever was behind that door. About the time Chulo fired, Chauncey let out a yell and flung himself to the side. He was none too quick because that shotgun went off right behind him. The shot hit the side of the car. The old man couldn't get the gun around to shoot in at me, and he never got off but that one shot. I don't know who got him, me or Chulo. All I seen was that shotgun suddenly come sliding down the crack and fall outside. Chauncey was on his hands and knees scrambling in the bushes.

"Let's get it!" I yelled to Chulo. "The gold."

We grabbed the three sacks and slung 'em outside and jumped after. Chulo slid the door shut while I yelled for Chauncey to bring the horses. He'd finally quit scrambling around in the brush and was heading around behind the station to get the horses. Up the train the engineer and foreman were coming down the steps of the cab. I fired a couple of quick shots in their general direction, and they scrambled right back up. Passengers had been sticking their heads out the windows of the chair cars, but they jerked them back quick enough when I fired.

Chauncey came running around the shack leading the three horses. Chulo and I ran to meet him, dragging the gold. I was just about to sling my sack up on my horse when I heard a gunshot behind me. I whirled and there was that damn fool Tom standing in the doorway of the car, holding a revolver in both hands and trying to get off another shot at us. I knelt and drew, but Chulo was quicker. He had his horse between him and Tom and he aimed over the saddle and dropped the clerk with one shot in the chest.

"Son of a bitch!" I said. My horse was jumping around from all the noise, and I was having trouble loading my sack of gold. Finally I poured about half of it in one saddlebag, spilling a few coins which I let lay, and then stuffed the rest, sack and all, into the other side. I swung up in the saddle. Chulo and Chauncey were just about loaded up. I took a quick glance up at the train in time to see some trainman come out of the cab with a rifle. Before he could kneel and take a shot I snapped off two quick rounds at him and he went flat. I didn't think I'd hit him.

Chulo was yelling "*¡Vámonos!¡Vámonos!*" He was mounted, and now Chauncey was swinging up.

"Let's go!" I yelled and turned and spurred my horse into the brush, quartering off into the southwesterly direction, rather than taking a direct route to where we'd hide out in the hills northwest of us.

We hammered through the brush, going pretty hard for a time. It was rough going through the mesquite and underbrush, and we'd get separated from each other for a minute or two when one of us would choose the other way around a particularly tough-looking clump of brush. Finally, when I figured we were a good two miles from the train, I signaled to Chulo and Chauncey to pull up. We needed to let the horses blow a little. We were going to have to push them to make our hideout as quick as we could. That train would be in Laredo before mid-afternoon giving the alarm.

We pulled up in a little clearing and got down. Our horses were blowing hard, their flanks heaving and slobber coming out their mouths around the bits. I was thirsty again, and I got my canteen and had a good drink then offered it around. Only Chauncey took some. Chulo, his face still tight against the pain, went to his saddlebag and got out a bottle of whiskey. He uncorked it, then took about four long drinks out of it. When he took it away from his mouth it was better than a third down. "Aaaaah," he said. "Aaaaaah!" He touched his eye.

"What the hell happened to your eye?" Chauncey asked him curiously.

"Never mind about his eye," I said. "Tell us what the hell happened back there at the watering station."

He hung his head and wouldn't look at me. "Awww, that," he said.

"Yes, that. How the hell did an old man get the drop on you?"

"Well—" he said. "Well—I mean—I had him. I took the station just like I was supposed to do. Had that old man under guard. Just like I was supposed to. Then I—" He faltered and stopped.

I waited, staring at him. Chulo was leaning against the horse. I could see from the way his face was beginning to relax that the whiskey was helping the pain some. But I was mainly concentrating on Chauncey.

"Hell, don't look at me like that, Will," he whined. "I couldn't help it, and we got the gold, ain't we?"

"I want to hear it," I said. "I want to know just how big a goddamn fool you are. I want to see if I can't figure out in advance just how you plan to try and get us killed next time."

"Well, goddamn," he said, flushing in the face. "I couldn't help it. I had that old man outside under my gun, just waiting for the train. Then he said he needed to go in the bushes and take a shit. So I let him. I—"

"You *what*?"

Chulo laughed.

"I let him go and take a shit. How was I to know? I was watching the bushes, but, hell, I didn't care if he run off. Fact is I'd just of soon he had. But he didn't. Next thing I know he's coming out of that shack with a shotgun and ain't nothing I can do, but drop my gun. But I never told him one word about you two coming

in on that train. I swear he figured that out all
on his own."

I turned around and looked at Chulo. He
was laughing without making a sound. Then
I looked back at Chauncey. I started to give
him a good cussing or knock him down or something, but it wouldn't have been any use. Finally I said, "Chauncey, you addle-brained idiot, I
got to put up with about one more week of your
society, and after that I'm shet of you, and if I
ever see you again it'll be my fault."

His face flamed again. "Well, that's a hell of
a thing for a man to tell his partner. I—"

I said dryly, "Don't call yourself my partner."

"Well, I'd like to know what else I was supposed to have done. Man asks to go in the
bushes and take a shit you've got to let him.
Hell, I didn't even know he had a scattergun
in that shack."

"Let's mount up," I said. I looked at Chulo.
"Whiskey help any?"

He tried to half-smile. "*Seguro*. Wheesky
always helps."

Chauncey wouldn't shut up. "Didn't I put you
on this gold? Didn't I? And ain't we got it? What
do you say to that, Mr. Wilson Young!"

"Mount up," I said.

But I couldn't keep a bad feeling against
Chauncey. I couldn't keep a bad feeling against
anyone. I had the gold. There was a bunch of
money in my saddlebags, and if I could stay hid
out for a week there wasn't a thing going to stop

me from crossing that border. I had pulled my last job. It was one hell of a good feeling.

We turned northwest now, riding slowly. As we went I said to Chulo, "I can't figure that damn clerk getting so brave all of a sudden. What do you reckon made him want to get killed over that gold for? Hell, it wasn't even his gold."

The black Mexican shrugged. "Maybe he didn't thenk he would get killed."

"Maybe not," I said. "But it was a damn fool thing to do."

"Well," Chulo said cheerfully, "at least his nose no longer pains him."

I looked at him. He was a mean son of a bitch all right, and no mistake. Side of his face was good swole up now, and I imagined his eye was near about to kill him. But he never let on other than to swig down a little whiskey every so often.

We spent the balance of the afternoon plugging away for the hideout, finally using the little town of Bandera to quarter off of for a guide to the place me and Chulo selected. It was hard to find, and we knew where it was. I didn't figure anybody else would find it unless they just happened to ride across it, though God knows what anyone would be doing riding through such country when there was easier going all around.

When we got to it we picketed the horses and then stowed what grub we'd brought in with what Chulo and I had packed in before. Then we laid our bedrolls up under the overhanging rock, and we were just about in business. We were going to be short on grain for the horses, and there wasn't much grazing about, but we weren't going to be using them, and they could make it on short rations for the time we'd be there.

Finally I taken my sack of gold and put it under my unrolled bedroll. The others did likewise.

When all that was done I got a bottle of whiskey, eased myself down in the shade, and had a drink. I was feeling pretty content. The job had turned out all right after all.

I awoke the next morning with the uneasy feeling that something wasn't quite right. As I come awake I lay in my blankets trying to think what it was was bothering me. We had the gold, we was good hid out, everything seemed like it ought to be in pretty good shape.

The sun was up enough to almost be over the little ridge that faced our camp. Chulo was already up, stirring around over a little fire making coffee. Chauncey was dead to the world in his bedroll. I threw my blankets back, and then I knew what was wrong. My side caught at me with a dull, aching pain. Not the sharp, almost good-feeling pain of a healing wound but a kind of dull, gray pain. I sat up slowly, and then I could feel the fever in my body and the ache in my joints.

"Oh, shit!" I said. I tore open my shirt and

jerked off the bandages, and I could see that the front wound, where the bullet had gone in, was already showing signs of infection. I couldn't see around to the back, but the hole still had a tent in it and ought to be all right. Not that it made much difference; it didn't take but one infection to do you in.

"Goddamnit!" I cursed. I got up and took off my shirt, shivering a little even though it wasn't very cool. I went over to the fire. Chulo grunted something, but I didn't speak. Instead I got a tin cup and poured myself up some of the coffee. The black Mexican was squatting on his heels, holding his cup with both hands and drinking slowly. The high smell of whiskey was mixed in with the aroma of the coffee so I knew he had his cup pretty well laced up.

"*¿Qué pasa?*" he asked me after I'd had a few sips of coffee.

I shrugged. "*No bueno.*" I asked him how his eye was.

He touched it with his hand. "I am aware it is there," he said, grimacing slightly.

"Get any sleep last night?"

He touched his wounded eye again. "This one likes it better when the other one is closed so it did not go so badly."

He was speaking about half-Spanish. I'd kind of noticed that his accent had gotten heavier, and he spoke more in Mex since he'd been hurt. I guess it took most of his strength to hold out against the pain and didn't leave him much left to work at the unnatural gringo language.

"I'll look at it right soon's I get some of this coffee in me."

"*No importa.*"

Then I grinned in spite of my side, which felt like it had a fire in it the way it was radiating heat. "But we got the gold, *chico.*"

He half-smiled at that. It was hard for him to smile because the swelling run all the way down the side of his face. "*Sí*" he said. "We have the gold."

After I finished my coffee I got a clean shirt out of my saddlebags and tore it up into strips. Then I sat Chulo down and took the dirty bandage off his eye. God, it was a mess. It was matted and swollen to where the eyelid was puffed way out. I wet a rag with some water from the canteen and wiped the matting away to see if he could open it. There was a little hole on the top of his eyelid, and I surmised that was where the lead fragment had come out, if, indeed, it had been a lead fragment that got him.

He couldn't open it so I took him by the hair of the head with one hand and, using thumb and forefinger, sort of pulled it open. Chulo jerked pretty good, but he didn't make no sound. I took a look at the eyeball, and it seemed as if there was a little cut along it. It appeared that the lead had come in at an angle, cut a little groove in his eye, and then went on out through his eyelid. If it had he was lucky. I couldn't see anything in the eye other than the cut, which was still spilling out fluid. I told Chulo to close his good eye and see if he could see out of the other one. He did for a second and then jerked his head away from me.

"It looks like milk," he said.

"Milk, huh." Hell, I figured he was blind for good in the eye. I said: "Chulo, ain't a damn thing I know to do about that eye. That's work for a doctor."

"Hell with it," he said.

"You're liable to lose it. May already have."

"Hell with it," he said again. "I got another one."

"Yeah, but that leaves you without no spares."

"I already lived half my life," he said, "I can make the rest of it on one lamp."

Oh, he was one tough *hombre* all right.

Chauncey got up, and we cooked a mess of breakfast, frying some bacon we had, then making corn fritters out of cornmeal and lard and water and frying them in the bacon grease. That along with the coffee made a good breakfast.

About mid-morning we all taken our gold and went out in the brush and cached it, each of us going in separate directions. I found me a big flat rock, scooped out some dirt under it, shoved my gold in, then moved the rock over the cache, marking it by taking a sight on the shoulder of a hill and lining it up with our camp.

We'd decided it was safest to hide the gold out. Though I felt we were safe, that wadn't no guarantee that some *hombre* might not just happen along.

I did all this with that bad, uneasy feeling in the back of my mind about my side. But I was trying not to think of it even though I was feeling a little more feverish all the time. Putrification of a wound was something I had occasion to know about, having seen men die of it, and I was considerably concerned. But since there was nothing I could do about it, except drink whiskey, I tried to keep it out of my mind and not worry. I'd examined the wound again, and even though it wasn't too red I knew that down inside something bad was working. I'd tried to pull it open and make it bleed, but all I'd gotten was a tiny drop or two, and I knew that wasn't going to help.

I'd drunk a considerable amount of whiskey. I'd heard that whiskey raised the heat in your body and helped kill infection, but I didn't know if that was so or not.

We were going to get low on whiskey I figured. We only had six bottles, and Chulo was going to need considerable, and I was going to need considerable. Either me or Chauncey was going to have to go into Bandera and get some more. I hated to send Chauncey, but I was afraid there was a chance I'd get recognized. 'Course I figured I shouldn't be afraid to let Chauncey go. Any fool can go straight into town and buy whiskey and bring it back. God, he had to be good for something.

Next morning I was feeling worse. I wasn't going to say anything about it to anybody so I got out of my blankets and creaked around as

best I could, rustling up some wood for the cook
fire and slicing the bacon. Chulo looked at me
kind of keenly a couple of times, but didn't say
anything. Chauncey, of course, wouldn't have
noticed it if I'd of had an ax sticking out the
top of my head.

We sat around after breakfast speculating
about what kind of hunt might be on for us.
I give it as my opinion that they'd expect us
to hustle for the border and would be concentrating down there.

Chauncey said, "Maybe we ought to have."

"Ought to have what?" I asked him.

"Lit a shuck for the border."

I frowned at him and looked at Chulo. "What
the hell is he talking about?"

The Mexican gave a shrug. "Who knows. Who
can say."

Chauncey said: "I'm talking about us sittin'
around here like this, like a bunch of goddamn
old women in a cave. Hell, I bet we could have
busted for that border and been across a-fore
anybody knew we was there."

"Are you crazy?" I asked him.

"Hell, I don't see why not. I'm gonna get
mighty sick of jest hangin' around here."

"You don't see why not, huh? Well, I'll tell
you. Just this once so you'll understand. See,
that train is a whole bunch faster than us, and
it would have been to the border about twenty-
four hours ahead of us. Which would have give
them time to get all nice and ready. 'Course
you'd probably figured on just riding across the

International Bridge with your gold I reckon." I
didn't even know why I was bothering to explain
anything to him. I guess it was because I was
feeling so bad it was easy for him to irritate me.
"You haven't got one lick of sense," I told him.
"Did you know that? Not one goddamn lick of
sense have you got."

"Take it easy, *amigo*," Chulo said to me. Then
he said in Spanish so that Chauncey couldn't
understand, "You are pissing into the wind."

Which was true enough, and I ought to have
known better.

I woke up the next morning feeling worse,
so bad that I could barely get out of bed. I
got off away from the others to examine my
wound. It was sending out red streaks, and
the wound itself was all angry and festering
looking. I thought that maybe if it capped over
and swole up I could lance it with my knife and
let the poison out. But, of course, I knew I was
going to get plenty sick before that happened.
My main worry was not dying, but not being
well enough to travel when it came time for us
to go. I couldn't very well expect the others to
hold up for me to get well, but it wasn't the kind
of ride a man makes the best alone. Not sick.

I came back to the fire. Chulo was watching
me pretty closely. He asked if I was feeling all
right.

"Yeah, sure," I said. I poured myself up a cup
of coffee and put whiskey in it. I drank that
down as fast as I could, and, after a few minutes, I could feel it helping. After that I made

myself eat some breakfast. I wasn't hungry, on account of the fever and all, but I knew I had to eat to keep my strength up.

We were getting low on whiskey, and I made the decision to send Chauncey in after it. I was too sick to go, and Chulo's appearance might have raised interest so that brought it down to Chauncey. I told him right after breakfast, and his face immediately lit up at the prospect of getting to go to town.

"No," I said. "You ain't going on any pleasure outing. I want you to go straight into town, buy six bottles of whiskey, and come straight back here. I don't want you to stop, I don't want you to talk to nobody, I don't want you to do nothin' except buy that whiskey and come straight back here. I don't want you to even take time to have a drink. Just get the whiskey and hightail it back here. Now you got that?"

He looked hurt. "You ain't got no call to talk to me like I was an idjet."

"I talk to you like you make me. Like you act."

"Hell, I ain't no fool, Will. You're shamin' me in front of Chulo."

"*You've* done the shaming yourself in front of Chulo. Now you just handle this job. Go on now, and catch your horse up and get on with it."

He went off grumbling to get his horse. We had hobbled them and turned them loose in the little gully where we're hid out. They were making do as best they could with the sparse grass, but they'd be wanting grain before the long ride we'd have to Mexico. Which give me a thought. When Chauncey came back with his horse I told him. "And see if you can't buy some grain for the horses. Buy as much as you can carry if they's any for sale."

Just before he left I told him: "Now I don't have to instruct you about being careful that no one follows you out of town, do I? Don't lead nobody back here."

He give me that grieved look again and mounted up. "Hell, Will," was all he said as he rode off.

I went over and squatted by Chulo. "I hate to do this," I said, "but we need that whiskey."

The black Mexican shrugged. "It'll be all right. There is no one in that little town who will take notice. This is not the country where you take notice of the other man's business."

"Hope to hell you're right," I said. "How's the eye this morning?"

"I think it goes better. There has not been so much pain." Then he laughed. "But I have stayed drunk, so it may have been hurting and I did not know."

I slipped his bandage and had a look at it. It looked some better. The eye was still very red and swollen shut, but some of the swelling was starting down along the side of his face. "Goddamn," I said, "this thing is looking better. You damn greasers must heal up faster than a white man."

He grinned. "Chili peppers and wheeskey. That is the Mexican's doctor."

"Bullshit," I said. But I didn't feel much like joking around. I could feel the fever rising every day, and, every once in a while, a chill would hit me and I'd shake with the ague. I knew I ought to have been in my blankets resting, but I didn't want to let on about the infection.

The sun got up, and it got good and warm. Me and Chulo went in to the shade under the over-hanging rock, and it was pretty cool in there.

Chulo looked at me once and asked, "Are all things *bueno* with you, señor?"

"Yeah," I said. "Sure, why not."

He looked at me. "You act a lettle seck?"

"Well, I ain't a lettle seck," I said, mocking him. But about that time a chill hit me, and I could feel my teeth wanting to chatter. I got up quickly and walked out in the sunshine.

Chauncey was a good long time coming back. It was three miles I figured to Bandera, and it shouldn't have taken him more than a couple of hours, but it seemed like he was gone closer to four. But, not having a watch, I couldn't be sure. Anyway, he'd brought the grain and the six bottles of whiskey.

I said to him, "Where the hell you been? Did you stop for a drink?"

"Hell no," he said, a shade too loudly. "Didn't you tell me not to? Mr. Wilson Young."

I felt like slapping him, but I was so weak with the fever I wasn't even sure if I could whip him. I said, "Watch your mouth. And go and get them horses in here so we can grain them."

"Why don't you? How come I got to do all

the nigger work around here? You or Chulo
do it."

Oh, he'd had more than one drink, and now
he was whiskey brave. I could see that I was
going to have to do something, but I didn't
know what. Hit him up side the head with
the barrel of my revolver was about all I could
figure. I was just about to order him to do it
one last time when I heard a distinct clink
from the ridge above and facing us. I whirled
just in time to see what I thought was a man's
head, wearing a hat, disappear below the top of
the crest. The sound I'd heard came distinctly
back to my ears as the sound of a shod hoof
on rock.

I turned to Chulo who'd been standing by.
"Did you see that?" I asked him, pointing to
the ridge. It was the top of the other side of
the draw we were down in. "I think I just seen
some *hombre* making off from here."

But Chulo shook his head. "I din't see nothing. You think you saw a rider?"

"I think I did," I said. But then I wasn't so
sure. I'd had a glimpse for an instant of what I'd
thought was a man's head, but I was so damn
feverish and weak I couldn't be sure my eyes
weren't playing tricks on me.

I asked Chulo, "Did you hear anything?"

He shook his head. "No, *chico*. But then my
hearing ain't been so good." He rubbed the left
side of his head. "She's all swole up."

Well, I could have heard it or I could have
imagined it. Or it could have been one of our

own horses making the noise. Still it had
occurred right after Chauncey got back from
town. As if someone had followed him back.

"I'm gonna have a look up yonder," I said. I
crossed the draw and began climbing the slope
on the other side. It was hard going the way I
was feeling, and I kind of half-climbed, half-
drug my way along by catching hold of bushes.

I got to the top and looked around. There
wasn't a thing in sight that looked like a man.
I watched a moment longer, looking off toward
Bandera, looking for movement. I didn't see a
thing.

Finally I said to myself: "Fever's got you
teched in the head, Young."

I made my way back down and told Chulo I
hadn't seen anything. Chauncey said: "Thought
I got followed, din't you? Well, I ain't quite as
stupid as you think I am."

"Nobody could be," I said. Oh, he was getting
pretty uppity and no mistake. I don't know if
the bastard could smell the sick weakness in
me or just what, but he was getting himself in
a fair amount of sass. I figured to allow him
just so much, then I was liable to shoot the
son of a bitch for lack of having the strength
to hit him.

Chulo and he finally went and got the horses
up, and we give them a good bait of grain and
then turned them back out.

It got plenty hot the balance of the day. I
laid in my blankets, burning up one minute

and then having a chill the next. My wound was looking awful. It was red and angry and swollen. There were red streaks coming out from it, and it throbbed with pain all the time. The only hope I had was that it was festering and I might could open it and make it drain.

That night I woke up sometime before dawn with a mouth as dry as sand and so hot inside I felt like I was scorching my clothes. I was so weak I couldn't walk, and I had to crawl over to where the canteen was. I got it opened and poured as much of it in my mouth as I could swallow. Then I struggled back to my blankets, taking the canteen with me. It was well that I did, for the water I'd drank was burnt out of me in five minutes and I was as thirsty as I was before.

Sitting up, drinking, I became aware of Chulo. He'd gotten out of bed and was standing there watching me. After a minute he came over to my bed. "You pretty seck, *amigo*?"

"Yeah," I said. I took a chill, and my teeth started chattering. "Yeah, it's my side. It done got infected."

"What you gonna do?"

"Nothing I can do, yet," I said, my teeth still chattering. "Might be I can open it up in a day or two. Right now I just got to tough it out. Go on back to sleep."

He stood there a minute more, looking like he felt he ought to do something, but he wasn't exactly up in his nursin' so he finally turned around and went back to bed.

I had deliberately kept myself from thinking about the girl, or the ranch, or any of the good things I hoped would be waiting for me in Mexico. I hadn't wanted to do it until me and the gold were safely on the other side of the Rio Grande. I reckon most men outside the law are pretty superstitious. I know I am, and I'd felt that if I thought about it too much I'd get my luck to running the wrong way. But that night, in the fever, I dozed and dreamed about the girl and what kind of life we could make. It seemed like it went on for hours. I'd doze off, then come to, then doze off, it going on until I didn't know if I was asleep or not. It was crazy stuff. A few times it seemed like Linda was so real I could have reached out and touched her. Then another time my whole horse herd run through the house I'd built for us and slam run over Linda. Then I'd dream that Linda has said yes about marrying, but that her daddy wouldn't let her, and I'd finally had to kill him. But then her mother had said no. It was awful stuff to have in your head.

Then, just about dawn, I woke up with my clothes soaked clean through with sweat. My fever had broke, and I was very weak, but clearheaded. I tell you that was some night, and I was damned glad to see the dawn.

Chulo was making a fire for the coffee, and I got up, put on my gunbelt and hat, and went over and sat down. I was so damn weak it was hard to walk. Chulo scolded me lightly for getting up.

"*Amigo*, you should rest. You pretty seck, I thenk."

"I feel better," I said. "I want to get some of that coffee."

Chauncey got up and joined us. "What's the matter with you, Will?" he asked me. "You're white as a sheet. See a ghost?" He laughed.

Chulo answered for me. "His wound has got the infection. He don't feel so good."

Chauncey looked at me curiously. "Couple more days and we'll be riding for the border. Hope you're well enough to travel."

That was Chauncey for you. But, hell, I didn't blame him. I might have felt the same way if it'd been him. But Chulo said:

"We don't go until the *jefe* is ready."

"Damned if that's so," Chauncey said. He was really feeling full of himself now that he had the gold. He'd forgotten how he had come by it.

Chulo just looked at him and didn't say a word.

"Don't worry about me," I said. "I don't feel so bad."

I got one of the little Mexican *cigarrillos* I like out of my pocket and lit it with a coal from the fire. I knew the relief from the fever was not going to last long. That infection would heat up again, and the only difference next time it broke would be that I'd be weaker. "I got to eat," I told Chulo. "I'm weak as a kitten, and I got to get some strength up."

"What you like to eat?"

I grimaced. "I wouldn't *like* anything. But I got to get something down. *Por favor*, please open me some of them beans, and I'll eat some beef jerky along with it."

He got up to fetch the food, and Chauncey said, "You never say *por favor* to me when you want something done. How come you talk to him one way and me the other?"

"Take a look at yourself," I growled at him. "Then you won't have to ask."

Chulo brought the can of beans and the jerky back. He was going to warm up the beans, but I told him to never mind. "I'm eatin' for strength," I told him, "not taste."

I cut the top out of the can and ate the beans cold with a spoon, eating some of the jerky along with it and drinking coffee. Then I ate a couple of cold biscuits we had left. The food made me feel better almost as soon as it hit bottom.

We were just sitting there, squatting around the fire, when I heard a noise from across the draw. Chulo looked up, and I whirled around.

There stood four men with drawn revolvers.

They were about thirty yards away, standing in a line. The one on the end to my left called out: "All right, raise up right slow 'n don't make no moves 'er we'll gun you down."

I immediately recognized him as the man Chauncey had called out for spitting on the floor when we'd been in the saloon in Bandera before. The others looked about like him, rough-dressed fellows with scraggly whiskers on their faces and dirty, snarled-up hair. They were trash, but they were trash holding revolvers at a very killing range. They shortened the distance by slowly advancing toward us.

The man from the saloon spit out a stream of tobacco juice. "Ya'll spread out thar," he ordered. "Don't be coverin' one and then the other 'n up. Git apart, damn ye!"

We fanned out in a line. They came on until they were about twenty yards away and stopped. The tobacco chewer was obviously the leader. He said: "Now take your hands and real kerful unbuckle them thar gunbelts off you'n and let 'em drop. Just real kerful like."

We did as we were told. My mind was racing, wondering what they wanted. I had a sick feeling inside me that they knew about the train robbery, knew about the gold, knew we were the men who'd done it.

When I'd dropped my gunbelt I said: "What do you men want? What's this all about?"

That seemed to tickle the tobacco chewer mightily. He snuffled out a kind of laugh. "You're funnin' me."

I insisted. "I want to know what the hell this is all about. Is this a robbery?"

It made him laugh again, a whinnying, snuffling sound. "Yeah, hit's a robbery. We're a-robbin' the thieves."

"What are you talking about?"

He waved his gun at me. "Jest cut out all the palaver 'n trot it out."

"What?"

"Gold, train robber. Gold. Now where'n hell do it be?"

"Shit," I said. "I don't know what you're talking about." Out of the corner of my right eye I could see Chulo and Chauncey. They were both standing quietly with their hands in the air. Chauncey was fidgeting around.

"Boy," the man said, "have I got to holt yore feet to the fire to git you to talk?"

"Won't do you any good," I said. "We don't know nothin' about no gold." I spit to show him my mouth wasn't dry, but I was feeling sick inside. If they were determined enough and willing to stop at nothing, they'd get the gold. Chulo would hold out a long time and I'd do all right, but Chauncey would break immediately and tell. He'd only be able to tell where his gold was, but that would be enough to keep the robbers going on me and Chulo.

"I guess they's nothing else for it," the leader said. "Let's go boys. We gonna have us some fun." They started forward.

In that instant Chauncey stepped forward. He took two steps toward them, pulled something out of his back pocket, and held it out to the men. "Hold it right there," he said sternly. "I'm law and these men are my prisoners. I'm taking—"

I didn't hear what else he said. It took me the briefest part of an instant to recover from my surprise, and then I dropped flat, sweeping my revolver out of the holster from where it lay on the ground as I did so. Lying flat I pumped two quick slugs into the tobacco chewer. He flipped over backward, some jerk in his arm causing him to sling his gun upward so that it made a high arc over his head. But I wasn't waiting to see. Guns were roaring all around. I leveled on the next man and dropped him with a carefully aimed shot in the chest. Chulo had dropped the end man on his side, but the fourth man had turned and was running up the gully. I tried a quick shot, missed, then got to my feet as he neared the top of the ridge, and fired and missed again. He got to the top and disappeared over it as I fired again.

"Oh, shit!" I yelled. "We got to stop him." I took off to my left, running up the draw. As I started I noticed for the first time that Chauncey was down. But there was no time to stop. I had to kill the man before he got away.

I sprinted down the draw until it narrowed then raced up the steep side of the incline. As I ran I was taking extra cartridges out of my pocket and reloading my gun.

I got to the top very winded. But there, twenty yards from me was the fourth man about to mount his horse. I took a quick shot, missed, and charged him. He was mounted now, and he slapped off a shot that hummed off a rock just in front of me. I pulled up, leveled down on him, and squeezed off a round. He backflipped off the horse, the startled animal running off a few yards and then stopping and looking back. I went up to the man. He was dead. I'd got him high center in his chest.

I suddenly felt very tired and weak. Whatever it was that had carried me along through the gunfight and then the run out of the gully had left me. It took all my strength just to walk back around the edge of the draw and down to our campfire. Chulo was bending over the three men we'd shot, looking in their pockets. Chauncey lay over near the campfire, one hand stretched out away from his body. Chulo looked up. "*El niño* is dead," he said.

"Yeah." I went up and knelt down by Chauncey. Chulo came up beside me. "I can't figure it, Chulo," I said. "I can't figure him doing what he did. What the hell was he doing, anyway?"

"*Yo no sé*," Chulo said. He didn't know.

Chauncey had just walked up toward them, pulling something out of his pocket and holding it out toward them. When I'd come up with my gun and they'd started firing they'd instinctively shot Chauncey first even though he didn't have a gun. It was him drawing the fire that had given me and Chulo time to cut them down.

His hand was clenched around something. I uncurled it. "I'll be goddamned!" I said. It was the badge from the marshal I'd killed. I reckoned that when Chauncey had gone back in the brush to hide the body, he hadn't been able to resist the badge. Though God only knows what he'd thought he'd ever do with it. I told Chulo. He didn't say anything.

"But even so," I said, "did he really think those *hombres* were going to leave because he had a tin badge? What the hell was he thinking about?"

Chulo shrugged. "Who can say? It is not possible to know the thoughts of a dead man."

"True," I said. "And I think it was impossible to know the thoughts of this one even when he was alive." I heaved a sigh and sank back on my heels. "But he shore saved our ass, I can tell you that. We'd be bacon right now if he hadn't done what he did."

"True," Chulo agreed.

"I got to get a drink," I said, "I'm about done in. Then I got to think."

I got up, made it in under the overhanging rock, and got a good drink of whiskey. It didn't help much. I was plenty weak, and I thought I could feel the fever coming back. I took the bottle of whiskey and went back to the fire where Chulo was squatting. For a while neither of us said anything, just sipped at the whiskey. I opened my shirt and looked at my wound. It was throbbing like hell. I longed to take a knife and drive it in my own flesh and let the poison out. The wound had bridged over, and the skin over the infection was tight and shiny. But it still would be too soon to lance it. I was going to have to ride out some more of the fever. Only it was going to be worse this time.

"Chulo," I finally said, "we got to get out of here. Those men," I indicated the *hombres* we'd shot, "will be missed, and somebody is going to come looking for them."

Chulo glanced at me. "*Amigo*, you well enough to ride?"

"No," I said, honestly. "But I got to do it anyway." I looked up at the sun. "I'll rest two, three hours, and then we take off."

"What about *El niño's* gold?"

"We can look for it," I said. "But I doubt if we'll find it. We ought not waste too much time on it. I'd like to be twenty, thirty miles away from here before morning."

"That's going to be pretty hard for you."

"Don't make no difference," I said. "It's that or sit here and die."

"Maybe be better you rest all day, then we ride out about the time it get dark."

I shook my head. "I don't reckon we better do that, Chulo. That's cutting it a little close. I figure somebody is going to be interested in these gentlemen's whereabouts a good deal of time before dusk."

I got a little more whiskey in me and then went up and laid down in my blankets. My mouth was gettin' dry again so I knew the fever was raging. Chulo went out and got the horses up and grained them. I figured we ought to do something about the horses the four dead men had ridden in on so I called to Chulo and asked him if he'd see to it. "Just unsaddle 'em and take their bridles off and turn them loose."

"*Seguro*," was all Chulo said. For sure. He was a good man. A good man in a fight and a good man to have for a friend.

I slept a little and got a little feverish. I

guess I'd been asleep an hour maybe when I
woke up from a hazy dream. But this time I
wasn't dreaming about Linda, I was dreaming
about Cata. I dreamed I was out in the middle
of the Rio Grande stuck on a sandbank with
my horse drowned, and Cata on the U.S. side
trying to throw me a rope. I woke up sweating
lightly with the dream in my mind. 'Course I
knew where that business about being in the
middle of the Rio Grande on a sandbank
came from. That's what had happened to me
and Les and Tod after we'd robbed a bank in
Carrizo Springs and were trying to get away
into Mexico.

I got up after a couple of hours and ate some
more beans and beef jerky and drank some
whiskey. Chulo had our horses up and loose
saddled and bridled and tied to some bushes
near the fire. He had Chauncey's horse on a
lead rope tied to his saddle horn. Chauncey
lay where he'd fallen, as did the other three
dead men. Chulo nodded toward Chauncey.
"You thenk we should bury him?"

I shook my head. "I ain't got the strength to
help you, and you don't need to be spending
yourself that way. Besides, in this hard ground
we couldn't give him nothing but a shallow
grave, and the cayotes would get him anyway."
I drank down a good slug of whiskey. "I appreciate what he did, but he's just going to have
to go unburied, bad as that sounds."

"He would understand," Chulo said, laughing
without humor.

"Shit he would," I said. "If his spirit's hangin' around here anywhere it's whinin' like hell because we ain't give the body a proper burial and said words over it and all of that."

Later on we had a look around for Chauncey's money, wherever he'd hidden it. We didn't make much of an effort, mainly because I was weak and mainly because we didn't think we had much chance of finding it. If we'd had more time we probably could have, but needing to get away as badly as we did we couldn't do much more than go off in the general direction Chauncey had gone when he'd hidden it and turn over a few rocks and look behind some bushes.

I don't think we minded much not finding it. We had plenty of our own, and then there's something about taking a dead partner's money. It's too much like robbing the body, and Chulo and I got a little too much class for that. Besides, it's bad luck.

So we give up on it and set about breaking camp. I was still so weak I wasn't a lot of help. But we loaded up our bedrolls and what food and water supplies we could carry and the whiskey and, of course, our gold money. When we were all ready I pulled up my cinch and then mounted. Chulo did likewise, taking Chauncey's pony on lead. I'd thought of taking one of the horses of the men we'd killed to have a spare, but I didn't think I wanted to be bothered with a horse on lead. Besides, one spare ought to see us through.

I hesitated before we left, looking down at Chauncey. It seemed goddamn hard to just ride off and leave him laying like he was. I wasn't going to pretend I'd liked him. I hadn't. If fact if my lot hadn't fallen to such a low estate there'd not have been any way I'd of been hooked up with such a fool as he. But, still, he'd come through for us at the last. I wondered if he'd realized he was going to lose his own life by his reckless play or if it had been like he'd done everything else; just on the spur of the moment, like a fool a-fucking, without fear or forethought.

But that wasn't a good thought to leave him on. So I took off my hat for just a second then put it back on and looked at Chulo. "Let's git," I said. We turned our horses and began making our way out of the little draw. It was coming mid-afternoon I figured.

CHAPTER 8

We rode southeast, pointing toward Eagle Pass, where I figured we'd try to cross. It was taking me away from my final destination in Mexico, Sabinas Hidalgo, where the girl lived, but to go otherwise would have meant crossing somewhere near Laredo, and we didn't want no part of that.

We rode all through the afternoon, taking it pretty slow, but keeping it going. I was hanging on as best I could, though a couple of times my head started swimming so that I damn near fell out of the saddle. I kept going by telling myself what a chuckle head I'd been to use the dirty rags for a bandage and that I deserved anything that happened to me.

Before dark the country had begun to change. We were gradually leaving the hard rock hill country and making it down into the rolling plains. The going was easier, but it presented us with the problem of where to hide if a catch party were to come after us.

We went on, until the moon was good up and until I couldn't make it any farther. Then we camped, graining the horses and putting them on picket ropes so we could catch them up at a moment's notice. We made a fireless camp, eating cold beans and jerky and biscuits and washing it down with whiskey and water. After we finished eating we sat, smoking. I was already in my blankets with my back up to my saddle. It was a warm night, but I was shivering and my teeth were chattering. Chulo tried to give me one of his blankets, but I wouldn't take it.

"You know," I said, "it's funny about this business."

"How so, *amigo*?"

"What happened to Chauncey. You just can't make mistakes in this game. If you do you'll pay sooner or later. I take it you recognized that gunman as the one that Chauncey called out in the saloon for spitting on the floor?"

"Aaaaaah," Chulo said, and I seen he hadn't realized it before.

"Yeah, it was him. Chauncey had to go and call attention to his self that time. Then when he rode in and bought that feed and whiskey, he was already a marked man, so he got followed back to see what he was up to. 'Course the word was all over this country about the train robbery and the gold we got away with. But Chauncey got himself killed two weeks ago when he made that mistake in the saloon by calling attention to himself. It was just waiting to catch up with him."

Chulo said: "I never took the look of it like that."

"Well, I have. Riding, I been looking over my last few weeks to see what mistakes I've made that are going to catch up with me."

"What you do?"

I said a little sourly, "Using that damn filthy rag for a bandage. Never thinking. The mistake didn't hurt me at the time, but it's shore hurting the hell out of me now. And it just might end up killing me."

Chulo said: "Aw, you ain't gonna die from that little wound. You too tough, *amigo*."

"Naw," I agreed, "I've about decided I ain't going to die from the infection, but it's got me so damn weakened down that if we was to get in a tight I might not be able to help myself as much as I generally can, and *that* might get me killed."

"Hell," Chulo said, "we make it. Don't worry."

But he sounded a little worried himself.

The country was still rolling; it hadn't flattened out completely as it soon would. Which was a good thing for us. Next morning, just as we were saddling up to leave, Chulo walked up on a little rise about fifty yards north of our camp to have a look around. I was kind of idly watching him, squatting on my heels drinking water and whiskey, trying to get the ache out of my bones. All of a sudden he dropped to the ground and then went to crawling backward. After he got below the crest of the rise he got to his feet and run, stooped over, back to the camp.

"Riders," he said tensely. He pointed toward a pretty good clump of mesquite. "We got to hide."

I never asked him nothing, just dropped my cup, took my horse on lead, and went crashing into the mesquite thicket. Chulo was coming right after me. I stood there panting from the exertion, trying to see through the sparse mesquite leaves.

Chulo said from somewhere over to my left, "They are maybe a half-mile away. Quartering toward the southeast."

We stood there watching the end of the rise Chulo had been up on. Pretty soon we saw a little band of horsemen emerge. There were six of them, and they were going at a slow trot. You could see that the man in the lead was studying the ground as they rode. We watched for a long time, and they kept going. When they were a good three or four miles away and almost out of sight over the horizon, we come out of the thicket leading our horses.

Chulo said, *"Mucha suerte."* Much luck.

"Yeah," I said. "Well, they were either lawmen or friends of that bunch we killed. Either way I don't want to run head on into them."

"No, it would not be good. How you feel?"

"It don't matter right now," I said. "We got to stack up some miles toward the border. Even though I don't know what's going to be waiting for us down there. But I got a feeling this country is working alive with folks looking for us. We better git."

We took off riding. I began to angle us a little more westward, just enough to give us a better edge on dodging pursuit, but not enough to greatly increase the distance to the border. I'd calculated we were about one hundred and twenty miles from Eagle Pass. In good times that would have been three days' hard riding. But with me sick it was going to take us considerably longer.

It was a rough day. The fever come over me strong after we'd ridden a spell. We stopped at a little creek to make a nooning and water the horses, and I told Chulo I was going to have to open my wound.

"It's got to come open, Chulo," I said, with the prairie dancing before my eyes in the bright sunlight, "or I ain't going to make it. We got to be on the lookout for someplace we can lay up all tonight and part of tomorrow. I figure it'll take me that long to recuperate, if the cutting does any good."

"*Seguro*," was all he said.

We slogged along, going through the mesquite and cactus and hot, still air. Even though it was just June the country was already starting to brown up from lack of rain. That was the problem with that country and why it'd never be good for much of anything. It seldom rained, and then when it did it come such a gully washer that it run right off before it could soak in. As I rode I got to thinking about all the miles I'd covered through the very terrain we were crossing. It seemed I'd been riding that country all my life, and it seemed that most of the time I'd been on the run with somebody chasing me.

I took a bottle of whiskey out of my saddlebags and had a drink, the fumes arising from the hot liquor nearly taking my head off. Chulo was leading, and I was riding about ten yards in the rear. Chauncey's horse was quartered out to the right and nearly abreast of Chulo. He was a bother because he kept trying to duck his head and graze, and Chulo had to constantly be jerking him along by the lead rope.

We were going in two gaits. We'd walk the horses awhile and then put them in a trot. It was a good way to cover ground without wearing the stock out. We couldn't afford to go any faster, for you never know, in our circumstances, when you might need a hell of a bunch of speed out of your mount, and you shore don't want him bottomed out beforehand.

But I dreaded it when we trotted. My horse had a pretty easy gait, but the trot still nearly fetched me each time. My side was just steady hurting. I'd had the pain so long and so regular that, even if I hadn't been weakened, it would have wore me down just holding myself in against it.

Toward sundown Chulo pointed up ahead. We could see a line of trees rising out of the prairie, scrub oak and willow. "The Frio River, I thenk," he said.

"Yeah." I came up alongside him. "But that little town of Cooncan is somewheres around here, and we don't want to get too close to that."

Chulo studied the trees. "It is west, I thenk," he said. "But I believe this would be a good place to hole up and attend your doctoring."

"Good as any," I said. "Though I wish we could make a few more miles." I knew the Frio to be about eighty miles from the border so we had only covered forty miles in two days of riding.

After another half-hour we got to the river. The copse lining its bank was pretty thick and made good cover. I just hoped we weren't too close to the town.

Wasn't much to choose from, the entire bank being about the same. But we finally chose a place above a steep bank and made camp. Chulo picketed the horses back in the trees. There was good grass back in there and plenty of it.

I drug myself around collecting wood for a fire. Chulo came back. "We better get on with this before it gets dark," I said. "You still got your frog sticker?"

"Of course," he said, smiling so that his teeth gleamed white in his black face. "*Siempre*." Always. He got it out and opened it and began stropping it on his boot top.

I spread my blankets and then took off my shirt and lay down. "Now hit her good and deep, Chico," I said. "You got to get it all." My wound was mounded up and tight and red and throbbing like hell. Even though the knife was going to hurt it would be a welcome kind of pain. I didn't know if the abscess was ready to be opened or not, but I knew I couldn't wait. I was already so light-headed from the fever I scarcely could keep my mind straight. While Chulo was heating his knife at the fire I got up and got a clean shirt out of my saddlebags to use as a bandage. The whiskey was already beside me, and I took a good, healthy pull from the bottle. Chulo came over, holding the knife out in front of him. "It's still plenty hot," he said.

"That's good. We'll cauterize it at the same time." I lay back. "Now hit it quick and deep."

"Of course," he said. He knelt by my side, and I explored the head of the abscess with a finger, searching for the sorest place. Finally I said, "About right here."

He put the point of the knife where my finger had been. He looked at me. "Ready?"

"Go," I said, and shut my eyes.

I felt the knife going in and in and in. But it hurt a whole hell of a lot less than I'd expected.

Chulo said, "Finis," and I looked. God, it just done my heart good to see how that thing was draining. Watching it I could feel myself getting better. It had been bad infected if a person was to judge by what was coming out. I lay there for a little while letting it drain. Then I turned over on my side so it would come out easier. Finally I got the whiskey bottle and told Chulo to hold the cut open. He'd made a good big one, and I give it one hell of a drink of whiskey. That nearly brought me to my feet. But I gritted my teeth and lay there shivering while that hot whiskey bit all through the wound.

When it was all burnt out I put a piece of the clean shirt over it for a compress then wrapped the long bandage around my waist to hold it in place, turned over on my stomach, and went to sleep. I felt weak and weary, but I could feel the fever going from me even as I started to doze. "Thanks, Chulo," I mumbled.

I barely heard him laugh and say, "Anytime, *amigo*."

I awoke sometime late that night. From the position of the moon I judged it to be two or three in the morning. I awoke clearheaded with the fever gone. I came stumbling out of my blankets only to discover I was still very weak. For a second, before I'd gotten up, I'd felt so good and so free of pain that I'd thought of waking Chulo and getting on the road for a few more miles. But once up I knew I needed more rest. I also knew I needed to eat. I found a can of beans and opened them and got some beef and some water. Then I took a seat on the little high bank overlooking the little clear river and ate with a better appetite than I'd had in a week.

It was pleasant sitting there in the night. The moon was shining on the water, and it looked silvered and shimmery. It was cool and the mosquitoes weren't even very bad. I took my time eating, letting my mind kind of wander aimlessly. I tell you, I was feeling better and more optimistic than I had in a long time. That period of being on the bum in Mexico had

near about been my undoing. It shames a proud
man to let himself get in the straits I'd fallen to
then, and I was near to getting down on myself,
a thing a man never wants to let happen. But
I knew I had been close. Seemed as if the low
estate I'd let myself tumble to had weakened
my pride and my resolution. Seemed as if I'd
quit being myself. Seemed as if I'd lost my con-
fidence to the point where it was beginning to
show.

Hell, I didn't want to think about those days.
They made me feel bad. But I'd hung on. I'd
damn near got to the end of my rope, but I'd
tied me a knot in the end and just hung on.
And now it was going to be all right. I had the
gold, and now, by God, I'd come back to being
Wilson Young. Well, we had us some miles to
make, but nothing was going to stop me from
getting to Sabinas Hidalgo. And once there I'd
deposit my money in the bank, set myself up for
a gentlemen horse rancher, and go to courting
that girl Linda. Listen, I'd waited a long time,
but now things were going to work out for me.

It gave me a happy frame of mind, thinking
on it. I sat there a few more minutes just letting
my mind play with all I was going to do, then I
got up and went back to my blankets and went
to sleep with the good feeling in my mind.

I awoke next with Chulo's hand over my
mouth. It had come good daylight. The air
was cool, and I could hear mockingbirds and
sparrows twittering away in the trees. I looked
up into his face. He was crouched low. "Sssh," he

said. He whispered, "Some mens are fishing."

Then I could hear their voices, just idle talking. Chulo took his hand away from my mouth, and I eased up on one elbow.

"They are in a boat, drifting," Chulo whispered.

We sat listening, and pretty soon I heard one of them say, "Let's put in here, Jake, and get out and stretch our legs a little. Just above the high bank looks like a good place to land."

I looked up at Chulo. "They're coming in. Sit and act natural. We're bound for San Antonio."

We both sat up, and I could see the little skiff. Two men were in it with handlines over the side, fishing for catfish I had no doubt. They got out the oars and pulled on over and run the boat up on the bank. They were perhaps fifteen yards upstream from us. I got up acting like I hadn't noticed them, and rolled my blankets and tied them behind my saddle. There was a little bloody flux on my shirt, but it didn't look too bad. I opened it and looked inside at the compress. It was soaked.

Standing up I felt pretty good. My side hurt, but it hurt good, like a healing wound. And I was stronger than I'd felt in days. I went over and poured myself a cup of whiskey then put a little water in it. It tasted mighty good. I stood there with Chulo watching the men get out of their boat and come up on the bank. They still hadn't seen us, though God knows why. Then they spotted our horses back in the trees. One of them said, pointing, "Look yonder. They's horses. Must be some folks about."

About that time they turned toward us and the start it give them was almost laughable. They were just old country folks, farmers or such. Weren't even wearing guns.

I said: "Howdy."

"Glory be," one of them said, "I didn't think they was a soul within a mile. Howdy, boys."

"Any luck on the fishing?" I asked politely.

"Some," the one said. They came on up the little rise to our camp. "Passing through?"

It was an improper question, but I said, "Yeah, heading for San Antonio."

"Long ride," one of them commented.

I offered them a drink and they took it. I didn't offer them another. Chulo stood around glowering. Having declared we were headed north we couldn't leave until they did.

They didn't seem to be in any hurry, seeming content to stand around and make palaver. Me and Chulo wasn't much help, not being really in the mood for small talk, but they didn't seem to need much help. I guess it would have bothered me, most times, but I was so damn happy to be feeling halfway decent that I wasn't paying much attention. Those old boys were looking over our gear and our horses, but they weren't asking any questions, which was damn smart on their part. They'd been hanging around fifteen minutes when I heard a whistle from Chulo who'd walked back into the trees to see about the horses. I told our visitors to make themselves at home and walked back to Chulo. He pointed out toward the plains. Far off, maybe two miles, I could see a bunch of riders heading our way. "We got to git," I said to Chulo. "Lead the horses up while I get rid of those two *hombres*." I whirled around and ran up to our camp. The two *hombres* looked up as I came running. I drew my revolver. "All right," I said, "the round-up is over. Get in your boat and get gone."

They kind of fell back, their eyes getting big in their heads. "Goddamnit!" I swore. "Get in that goddamn boat and get the hell out of here. Move!" I cocked my revolver.

That fetched them. Without a word they turned and began scrambling down to where they'd left their boat. Shooting me frightened glances they shoved it in the water and jumped in, unshipping the oars. "Now listen!" I said harshly. I'd followed them on down. "I want you to get on *down* this river and I mean I want you to get down it in a hell of a hurry."

They were rushing. I said: "You better be out of my sight in five minutes or I'm going to commence letting off this cannon, and it generally goes the way I point it."

They never made a sound, never asked me what had happened, nothing. They just laid into them oars and started pulling downstream. I stood there watching until they went around a bend and out of sight. I figured the start I'd give them would keep 'em going for at least a mile or two. And that would get them out of the way of the catch party, if it was such, so they couldn't be asked any questions about the two men they'd just seen and which way they were headed.

I turned around and went back to our camp. Chulo had the horses up, had his saddled, and was smoothing the blanket on mine.

"They still coming?" I asked.

"*Sí*" he said.

I saddled my horse and then began loading our equipment while Chulo tried to erase as much of our sign as he could. I mounted up, checking my pistol load when I was in the saddle. "Let's go," I said to Chulo. "They're going to know we been here anyway. What we need to do now is get us a little distance."

He mounted up, and we rode upstream looking for a good place to cross. The Frio was just a little, quiet river no more than fifty yards wide and about breastplate deep on a horse. We found an easy place and crossed without incident.

When we got to the other side and made it through the trees, I said, "Let's lift 'em up."

We put the horses in a slow gallop, pounding through the rough country as best we could. We weren't worrying about tracks. Tracking in that country ain't real easy and takes time. Them boys could either track or chase us. Either way they were going to come up with nothing more than sunshine and lathered-up horses.

After what I calculated to be about three or four miles of hard riding we pulled up and got down and walked, leading the horses. They were blowing and sucking air, but they were both iron hard and could take a good bit of tough riding. Chulo looked pretty tired. He'd had a rough time of it with the extra horse who'd kept getting bushes and mesquite trees between him and Chulo and getting the rope tangled up.

We made a fireless nooning, eating apricots and beef right out of the cans while we held the reins of our horses. I had a good drink of whiskey and then lay down on my back and took the compress off my wound and gave it a drink too. It burned enough to let me know the cut was still plenty fresh, but the wound was looking some better. All the redness in my side was gone, and it felt like a wound will when it's healing.

Before we rode out Chulo took the bandage off his eye and threw it away. I asked him what he'd done it for. "It bothers me," he said. I took a look at his eye, and it looked some better except the eye itself was still swollen shut. I prized it open. Chulo didn't wince much so I guess a lot of the soreness had gone out of it. The eyeball didn't look good. It was commencing to get cloudy like you'll see in a blind cow or horse's eye. I told Chulo about it. "I'm afraid you've lost that lamp," I said.

He shrugged and mounted up. "*Mala suerte*," was all he said. Bad luck.

We took off in a slow gallop and then gradually pulled the horses down to a walk, though a fast walk. Every so often I looked over my shoulder, but there was no sign of pursuit.

Which didn't mean that catch party couldn't be a few miles back, just over the horizon.

We kept up the pace, and that evening just at dusk we saw the town of Uvalde off to our left a mile or so. Lamps were already being lit as people got ready for the night.

It was at Uvalde where we'd tried to rob the Cattleman's National Bank that some bad things had happened to me. There'd been me and Les and Tod and Howland Thomas and Howland's running mate, the Mexican Chico. Chico had got killed inside the bank, and I'd had to kill Howland later when he'd tried to run out on us and, of course, Tod got himself lung shot when we was making our getaway under a hail of bullets. On south of Uvalde was the town of Pearson, where we'd tried to get Tod a doctor without success and where he'd died down in the little sandy wash beside the creek bed. We'd buried him there in the sand, and Les had taken Tod's Bible to return it to his daddy and tell him what had happened. Only Les never got there, being killed by Morton and Bird down in Laredo.

Oh, that part of the country held some memories for me all right. And most of 'em bad.

I said to Chulo, "Better'n halfway."

"I am for Mexico," Chulo said. "I want to rest and get drunk and have no one chasing me for just a leetle time."

"Me and you both, *amigo*," I said. Then I asked him what he was going to spend his money on.

He shrugged. "Who can say? Perhaps as I always do. On wheesky and the women and having a good time."

"Not me," I said with emphasis. "I'm going to buy me a spread. I'm through with this outlaw business. I've pulled my last job."

Chulo didn't say anything, but he turned in his saddle and grinned at me.

"I mean it," I said.

"Of course," he answered.

We rode in silence for a time, and then I said: "When we get good and clear of Uvalde I reckon we ought to camp for the night. These horses can use the rest. They's a creek on up here about four or five miles, and we can pass the night there."

"As you say," he said.

We passed Uvalde as it got good dark. Well, I could see why Chulo wouldn't believe me when I said the train was my last job. Uvalde was to have been my last job, too, but, of course, it hadn't come off. Looking off to the east toward the lights of the town it seemed like some way long time in the past that the five of us had come riding into that bank. But it hadn't been that long in years, no more than two. And if I could say anything in truth it was that those years had not been good ones. Had been, in fact, the two worst of my life. There'd been times down there in Mexico when I'd despaired of things ever going right again. But I guess that happens to a man when he passes thirty and feels himself starting to get old and slow.

In what had been my line of work there ain't no room for hands who are old and slow. But now, now that I was finally going to get in the legitimate business of ranching, thirty didn't seem so old.

The sky was clear and there was a good moon out. We kept on until I saw the scraggly line of trees that trailed along beside the little creek.

"Just ahead," I said to Chulo. We were both plenty tired and glad to be getting to a place where we could rest.

I didn't see the fire until we got closer. I guess it had been hid by a clump of trees and only swung into our line of vision as the angle changed. "Oh, shit!" I said to Chulo. "Somebody's already there."

He swore softly in Spanish as we came to a halt. I studied the fire and the trees. 'Could be something or it could not," I said. "But we can't take the chance. Only thing is we *got* to water these horses or they are going to crater on us."

"What you think we do?"

"We'll turn up east," I said. "Water the horses and then put a little distance on these folks."

"*¿Cómo no?*" Chulo said tiredly. Why not.

I told him to dismount, that we would walk and he should keep his horse between himself and the fire. "That way, if they see us, they might think it's just a few horses coming to water."

We got down and walked over the rough ground. My feet were sore and tired from the walking we'd already done. Fortunately the wind was blowing out of the west so that their horses couldn't smell us, nor ours theirs, and whinny.

It took us about half an hour to quarter way up the creek from the fire and get in through the trees. We did so without incident, coming to the bank, loosening the horses' cinches, and then letting them drink. I lay down on my belly and put my head underwater, letting its coolness revive me a little. I got to my feet and looked at the moon, figuring it to be around 10 or 11 P.M.

We had a drink of whiskey, not taking the chance on smoking, then cinched the horses up, mounted, and splashed across the little creek. On the other side we got down and started walking again, figuring on doing that until we were good clear of the creek.

"Damn," Chulo said, yawning. "*Amigo*, I could sleep now, I tell you that for the truth."

"Myself, pad'nuh. I'm about froze I'm so tired."

We were no more than three or four hundred yards from the creek when I happened to glance back toward the fire and saw little winking flashes. In another second the crack of rifles reached my ears. "*¡Vámonos!*" I said.

We swung into the saddle and put our horses into as hard a run as they could manage, tired as they were. But this was no time to be saving horseflesh, and we laid on with spurs and squirt, driving the animals faster and faster.

I took one quick look over my shoulder but couldn't see any pursuit coming. Finally after about a mile I felt my horse really beginning to labor, and I called to Chulo to slow down. We dropped down to a walk, and I turned in the saddle to look back. I could still see the creek, the line of trees like a dark mark on the earth, but I couldn't see anything that looked like horsemen. I shook my head. "I don't know what that was, some liquored-up old boys firing at anything or real trouble. But I do know we got to rest these horses or we'll soon be afoot."

We got down and began the painful job of walking over the rough ground. I kept looking back ever so often, but they was still nobody coming.

"Shit!" I finally said. "That was a bunch of damn fools. Hunters or such. Probably thought we were deer or longhorns. Just shot their rifles off and damn near caused us to founder these horses. I don't know whether to be glad it wasn't the law or not."

We kept walking and then all of a sudden Chauncey's horse just up and kneeled over on his side.

"What the hell!" I said. I went over to where the horse was laying without moving. At first I figured he'd foundered, but then I saw the hole high up on his shoulder. He'd been shot and had died on his feet. "Well, I be go to hell," I said to Chulo. He came over and studied the wound and began to swear in Spanish about losing the horse. "Wait a bit," I said. "Wait a bit. If that bullet don't hit the horse it's liable to hit you."

He thought about that for a moment and then finally grinned. "Yes that is perhaps right. And I prefer that the horse be shot than myself."

We took the lead rope off, and Chulo coiled it and put it back on his saddle. We went on.

We kept on for another couple of hours, walking awhile and then mounting and taking it slow and easy for a spell. Sometime after midnight we found a clump of mesquite that give good enough cover for us to bed down in. We didn't bother with our bedrolls, just lay down on the ground with our horses' bridle wrapped around our wrists, and slept like dead men until dawn.

We made another cold breakfast next morning, warming ourselves as best we could with whiskey. I figured the Rio Grande was only about forty miles away, a day's ride for a determined man. But our horses were played out and wouldn't take hard riding, so I calculated we'd make it an easy two-day trip.

We grained the horses and then mounted and set out at a walk. Going along Chulo said: "You ever thenk of my cousin's sister?"

"Sure," I said, a little startled at him bringing it up.

He said: "She was *mucho* taken with you."

"Yes," I said.

"She even spoke to her brother of it."

I was surprised. "It went that far, huh?"

"She is a fine woman," he said.

I agreed. "Yes. Very fine."

"Even if she has been with a few men. But that is of no importance. She would be a good woman for a good man, I thenk."

I almost laughed. It sounded as if Chulo were pleading her case with me. I had never told him about Linda, never told anyone, for that matter, except Les, and there was no way for him to understand what I'd been working for, what I was heading for, and what I hoped to possess in the near future.

So I said nothing.

Chulo let the subject drop and we rode on.

We made another fireless camp that night, the last camp, I hoped, that I'd be making north of the Rio Grande for some good while. I guessed us to be only about fifteen or twenty miles from the border and figured we should strike it a few miles east of Eagle Pass.

We were both so tired we had trouble going to sleep, so we laid there a time in the still night drinking whiskey and talking in low tones. Around us were sounds of the prairie, the quiet chirp of crickets, the ground wind blowing through the mesquite trees and rattling the dried beans that hung from their branches.

"I been thinkin' about Chauncey today," I said.

"No use in that," Chulo answered. "He dead."

"Oh, I just been thinkin' how young he was. He was a damn fool, but I wonder if we weren't all damn fools when we were his age. Maybe he wouldn't have been if he'd got a chance to grow up."

"He be a damn fool now, he always be a damn fool. He was old enough."

"I know," I said. "Still, I don't reckon he ever got a chance to find out what he wanted to do. In a way he reminds me of myself. I just more or less drifted into the robbing business because I didn't know any better. I kinda got the idee he did the same thing."

"*No es mismo,*" Chulo said. It's not the same.

"Maybe not," I said, "but I still feel bad about him. I was pretty rough on his old ass, you know. Treated him like a schoolboy. Maybe if I'd gone out of my way to teach him a few things he might not have been such a damn fool."

"I thenk," Chulo said gently, "that you make the wheesky talk. A man like that you can do nothing to help. You feel bad because he was killed in saving the two of us. If he had been killed in one of his foolishness you would not have felt this way."

I thought on that a minute and decided Chulo was right. "Yeah," I said, "to hell with it."

We were up and riding not too long after dawn. I grew more and more apprehensive as we approached the border. I truly expected there to be patrols out, and my plan was to stop short and wait for dark and then cross then. But the closer we got the harder it was for me to hold myself back. I wanted into Mexico, and I wanted in there right away and no mistake.

We took it slow, saving our horses in case we should have to run for it. I was able to judge our nearness to the border by the way the country began to gradually green up. They get more rain, for some reason, right down along the river than they do in either direction away from it.

"Hope that old river is shallow," I told Chulo nervously. "We ain't going to have a whole hell of a lot of time to be prowling up and down it looking for a place to cross."

"It has not rained," Chulo said.

"Not here," I agreed, but I was thinking about the time we'd caught it on the rise when the rain had been way upstream.

We come on and on, not seeing a soul, until we finally topped a high bluff, and there was the Rio Grande, which they call the Rio Bravo in Mexico, right below us. I calculated we were some three miles east of the two border towns of Eagle Pass and Piedras Negras.

"There it is," I said.

"Sí," Chulo said.

I looked at it for a second and the land on the other side. Then I reined my horse around to the east. "Let's try this way a bit. Looks like the land slopes off better."

We rode downstream until the bank sloped off and we could ride down to the river's edge. It didn't look bad at all, maybe a hundred and fifty yards wide, brown, slow-moving water swirling along. We kept cantering along east, looking for a good place where we wouldn't have to get out of the saddle and swim. Finally we rounded a bend, and there was a place, where the river narrowed, that looked plenty shallow. It was kind of rapids, though not all that swift, where the river run over some rocks. We could see that it was a couple of feet deep at the most. "This ought to be all right," I said. We urged our horses forward and crossed without incident. In five minutes I was standing on Mexican soil. I looked over at Chulo and laughed. "Hell," I said, "we're here."

He grinned hugely, those white teeth showing up big in his black face. God, I tell you he was a sight. He hadn't shaved in a week and with that eye swole shut he looked like one bad *hombre*. I reckoned that, except for the eye, I looked every bit as bad.

We rode on back into a shady bunch of live oak and mesquite and dismounted.

"Let's have a drink," I said. I got two bottles out of the saddlebags and passed one to Chulo. Then I held mine up, and Chulo clinked his against it. "Here's to luck," I said.

We always drank to luck. People in our line of work always do.

I lit up one of those little *cigarrillos* and Chulo did likewise. We squatted on the ground, smoking and drinking and not saying much. I calculated it was just after one o'clock. We hadn't made a nooning for the both of us had been in too big a rush to get across the river.

"Well," I finally said, "what you reckon to do?"

"I am for Piedras Negras," he said. That means black rocks in Mexican.

"I'm heading on into the interior," I said. I didn't say where because I didn't want any of my old riding partners to know where I was going because word will get around. I was all through with my past life, and I didn't want any of it coming back to plague me. As far as the people in Sabinas Hidalgo were going to know, I would just be a medium well-to-do gringo who'd decided to go into the horse business there in their pretty little town.

"Got anything going in Piedras?" I asked.

He shook his head. "Some family and friends. I intend on doing nothing for the immediate time, but to be very lazy and to drink great amounts of wheesky and fuck all the women I can. I will also sleep a great deal. The train robbery was very successful, but I was not permitted to sleep the amount I am accustomed to."

"Damn straight," I said. "I can see what a hardship that was on you." I hefted my bottle and held it out for a toast. Chulo clinked his and waited for me to say the words. "To Chauncey," I said. "Who was a damn fool kid, but who was right as rain about the gold and who got hisself killed in as good a way as he could have wanted."

"Very well put," Chulo said. We drank. Chauncey was still one ghost I hadn't been able to put to rest. I don't know why I should have felt responsible for him, but I did. Maybe it was because he reminded me so much of Tod.

We talked awhile longer, just aimlessly, laughing over some of the good times we'd had, carefully avoiding the bad. Which is the way it's done. When a job has ended well you don't talk of what went wrong, but of how well you came through it. Finally Chulo stood up. "*Me marcho*," he said. "For Piedras Negras."

I stood also. "Yeah, I got to get kicking myself."

Then Chulo put out his hand, and we shook and he mounted and rode off. That's the way it is with us. We had rode together and robbed together and risked our lives together, but when it come time to say good-bye it was just like that, "Adiós and *buena suerte*." Good-bye and good luck. And never look back.

I stood there a little longer, holding my horse and drinking whiskey. Then I corked the bottle and put it back in my saddlebags. I hesitated long enough to have a look at the gold. It was still there, gleaming and solid. It looked like a train ticket to where I wanted to go. I closed the flap and buckled it and got on my horse and started east. I was safe. I was back in Mexico with the money.

CHAPTER 9

I reckoned Sabinas Hidalgo to be about one hundred and fifty miles away. I was going to take it plenty easy because me and my horse both were about bottomed out. There wasn't much on the way. The first town I'd come to would be Guerro, about fifty miles southeast, then would be Anhuac, another sixty, and then I could either go on into Sabinas or detour slightly south through Lampozas. But I had plenty of supplies, and the only reason I'd want to stop in a town would be to sleep in a bed. Of course there was the matter of the gold. In a town I couldn't carry it everywhere with me so I'd either have to stay in my room or run a risk of somebody breaking in and robbing me. A risk I was not about to take.

After I got away from the river a couple of miles the country was pretty dry and brown. It was also hot, very hot. Me and my poor horse were both sweating hard after just a few miles of travel. The country was flat with the same trees and underbrush as was on the other side. Overhead there wasn't a cloud in the sky, nothing except the sun.

I stopped that evening before dark and made camp. The first thing I did was to take my gold a little ways away from the fire and hide it. I was in Mexico all right, but that didn't mean there weren't plenty of bandits around who would have liked to get their hands on that sackful of double eagles.

I built a small fire to warm up some supper then extinguished it before I turned into my blankets. There was no point in calling attention to myself.

Before I went to sleep I lay there and stared up at the sky, thinking about the time just past. I had the gold all right, but the getting of it shore played havoc with some people's lives. I'd killed that town marshal, Chulo killed the money car clerk, either me or him had killed the old man at the watering station, Chauncey had got himself killed. Not to mention the four *hombres* who'd tried to rob us. That made eight and I'd killed four for sure. It did no good to ruminate on such things, but killing has always made me feel bad. Especially, outside of Chauncey, the money car clerk. I still couldn't figure what had possessed him to come up with that shooting iron as we were leaving. The only thing I could figure was that he was more scairt of the railroad than he was of us. But with the railroad all he'd lost was his job. Finally I quit thinking on it and went to sleep.

Next day I raised Guerro and went on into town. At first I was going to go in a *cantina* and have a sociable drink, but once I dismounted and put my saddlebags over my shoulder I realized the gold was too heavy to walk around with. So I retied it behind my saddle, pulled up the cinch, and rode on out.

Well, it felt a little strange to be riding alone after a month of having two partners. But I'd been riding alone for the last two years so I guess it wasn't no surprise. Still it was not as comfortable at camp, not having anybody to talk to as it had been. Consequently I found myself riding later and getting up and leaving earlier. Riding, I found myself thinking on something I didn't even want to admit to myself. It is difficult for a man as hard as I was to admit to himself that he yearned for a wife and a home and maybe children. That he yearned for a little comfort, a little softness, a little feeling of belonging. But it was there, there in my mind, always laying just a little bit below the surface. And now with the prospect nearer to hand, I was having a hard time keeping it submerged, something I'd been able to do the majority of my life. And I knew it was wrong and a mistake to let myself get built up, to let myself get excited over the prospect of at last settling down. I had learned, a long time ago, not to count your money you've taken out of the bank until you've made your getaway. But here I was, riding along in the lonely country of northern Mexico, and I damn near already

had the ranch house built, Linda pregnant, and
the horse herd ready to sell off its first crop of
yearlings. I fought myself on it, trying to hold
off such castles in the sky until I had made
more progress toward my goal. Didn't do much
use. All it did was make me ride faster.

I raised Sabinas Hidalgo on the morning of
the fourth day. You come into Sabinas from
the east over a crop of low hills. You come
riding through that brown, parched-out country and then you top a hill and there it is, the
town and the long, wide valley it's set in. It's
a pretty sight. The valley seems to be green all
year round, and Sabinas is maybe the cleanest
Mexican town I'd ever seen. All of the houses
seem to be whitewashed adobe or limestone
with red-tile roofs. The buildings downtown are
granite and marble, and the streets are wide,
and some are cobbled with flagstone and some
with brick. The town has got a bunch of trees
in it, too, and the people, even the poor, don't
seem as greasy and run-down as they do in most
of Mexico. Altogether it's a might prosperous-
looking little town.

I took my horse gently down off the line of
hills and rode on into town. I'd put up at the
Mirador Hotel when I'd been there before, and
I didn't see no reason to change. As I rode
through the town I observed the plaza where,
one Sunday, I'd watched Linda and her sisters
on the promenade. I'd been across the street,
and I'd stood there, already in love with her
since I'd seen her at her uncles, and just damn

near eat my heart out. Well, that had been a long time ago.

I got to the Mirador, turned my horse over to a boy to take down to the livery stable, then took my saddle and saddlebags on into the hotel. It was a fine hotel; big heavy furniture in the lobby and a good saloon with a big long polished bar where all the landed gentry seemed to make it a habit to meet of an afternoon. I walked through the lobby with its high ceiling and went up to the desk and checked in. The first thing I wanted was a bank, and then I wanted a bath. The clerk said there was a bank a couple of blocks down the street, and I booked a bath for later on that day. I sent the boy up to my room with my saddle then I turned and went out, hauling that gold. I tell you I wanted to get shut of that load. I was getting damned tired of carrying it around and guarding it.

The bank was the Banco de Nacional, a big, imposing, granite building of two stories on a corner. I went on in and told one of the clerks I wanted to see the *jefe*, the head man. He looked at me kind of sharp and I couldn't blame him. I reckoned I looked more like I'd come to rob the place than to make a deposit. Besides that it was a pretty high-toned place, quiet, everybody seeming to be speaking in whispers, and elegant furniture and marble floors. But the clerk went away and came back with a severe-looking, middle-aged gentleman sporting a big handlebar mustache. He said he wasn't the manager, but the assistant manager, and could he help. I figured that would be all right, and we repaired to a desk in his office, and I clumped down the saddlebags and said I wanted to deposit the money. Well his attitude changed right quick when he seen the amount of deposit I wanted to make. I let it slide, having seen his kind before and knowing their ways. He got me a chair right quick and pressed a cigar on me and lit it. I sat there smoking that cigar and enjoying myself while he counted the money. It was some change for me, to be putting money in a bank instead of taking it out. I tell you, it made me feel plenty good with myself. For the first time I was starting to feel solid about my chances for getting off the owl hoot trail and living like civilized people.

The money come to fourteen thousand seven hundred and sixty-two dollars. Me and Chulo hadn't got it split exactly, but we done the best we could. I taken two hundred for pocket money, and he gave me a deposit receipt for the rest and had a boy in to sack up the money and put it away. Then he folded his hands on his desk and asked me how else they could help me.

Well, I'd been expecting that. I had me a story ready because I knew anything I told them at the bank would be pretty common knowledge on the street in a short while, and I wanted to get off on the right foot. I told the banker that I'd been ranching up in north Texas and that I'd sold the place and had come here with the intentions of going into the horse-raising business if I could find the right piece of property and put the other loose ends together.

Well, this was better than he'd expected. Not only was I someone with money, I also wanted to spend it. He beamed like he had about half a load on and said the bank did a little land brokering and maybe after I was settled in at the hotel, I could come back and we could discuss what was available. I said that, yeah, I could do that, but that first I needed to go out and visit with Señor de Cava. Well, that taken him up short, me knowing a first-class citizen like the don. Of course he never let on, but I could see him giving me an appraising look and maybe deciding I was worth even more than I'd seemed to be.

After a while I made my adióses and went on back to the hotel and had my bath. They done it first class, bringing the big wooden tub right into my room and filling it up with hot water and then keeping the water coming while I soaked. Lord, it felt good. I hadn't had a bath in a good little while, and I was getting to where I near about couldn't sleep with myself.

After that I went out to buy some new clothes. I put on the cleanest ones I had, but they still felt dirty after my bath. But I walked along in the afternoon sunshine enjoying myself and feeling pretty good about things. There was a considerable number of people on the streets going about their business, and I got to wondering how old Chulo was doing. It was likely that I'd never see him again, but he was a good man, and I was glad he'd been part of my last job. Every once in a while I'd catch sight of some Mexican beauty in a white lace dress and my thoughts would go to Linda. It was my hope that I'd be seeing her the next day. Of course I wasn't going to rush it. I was going to get in damn solid with her daddy before I ever even acted like I was coming courting.

I found a good clothing shop and bought me some fancy duds. Main thing I got was a pair of flared brown britches made out of some soft kind of cloth. Then I got me a frilly kind of white shirt to wear with them and some new boots. I bought some other britches and shirts, but I didn't buy a new hat. Man has a hat a long time he'll wear it until it just about gives up. It takes considerable time to get a hat to fit itself to your head so's you don't even know you're wearing it. My old one was sweat and travel stained, but it was still good enough for me.

I put on a new pair of britches and a shirt in the clothing store as well as my new boots and just told the man to throw away my old stuff. Back out on the street I walked along feeling good to be clean and rigged out in new stuff. I stopped at the plaza and sat down and smoked for a while, thinking to myself that I was liking this new way of living. Hell, I could even write drafts on a bank. Something I never figured to see myself doing.

I went back to the hotel and got paper and pen from the clerk and took it over to a little

table in the corner and composed a note to
Señor de Cava. It wasn't much, I just com-
mended myself to his memory if he recalled
my previous visit, said I was in town again
and would like to come out the next afternoon
if that was convenient. Then I hustled me up
one of the boys around the hotel and gave him
a peso and the note and told him to take it to
Don de Cava and bring back a reply if there
was one.

I didn't have anything to do after that so I
walked down to the livery stable and checked
on my horse. Finding him all right and being
well cared for I went on back to the lobby and
sat around smoking. Now that the note was
gone I commenced to get kind of nervous. What
if de Cava was out of town? I sat there imag-
ining every bad thing I could think of until I
finally had myself as jumpy as a long-tailed cat
in a room full of rocking chairs.

"This won't do," I said to myself. So saying
I got up and went into the bar to get myself a
drink and see if I couldn't cut more sign on the
town and the country thereabouts.

There were several gentlemen sitting at a
table, and there was one man at the bar.
The men at the table were well dressed and
were either ranchers or prosperous business-
men. They appeared to be drinking coffee and
brandy. The man at the bar was dressed well
in a brown suit of clothes with a white sash
around his waist, but he was fat faced and
paunchy and looked pretty drunk. He was

hunched over his drink staring at the bar. He had sweat on his face.

I bellied on up to the bar at the end and told the bartender to give me a glass of his best bourbon. Then I turned to look the gentlemen at the table over. They were talking like all Mexicans do, heatedly and with a lot of arm waving and fidgeting. I swear, I sometimes believe you could watch two Mexicans discussing the time of day and you'd think they were about to go to war. Watching, I sipped at my bourbon and wondered how long it would be before the boy got back with my answer.

Then I heard the drunk down the bar say, "Fucking gringo!"

It kind of startled me. I looked down the bar at him without any idea he was talking about me. But he was staring me right in the face. "Fucking gringo," he said again, only this time he said it louder. The gentlemen at the table had heard him and they got quiet and the ones with their backs to the bar swiveled around in their chairs to see what was going on.

Well, I didn't quite know what to do or say it had taken me so by surprise. I figured I'd just ignore the man. But he wasn't going to have that. He pointed his finger at me and said. "You! You fucking gringo!"

I looked at the bartender who was busily wiping the bar and not looking at either one of us. The man kept pointing his finger at me. He spoke pretty good English, but his speech was slurred by the whiskey he'd drank. "Big

gringo," he said. "Big gringo. Fuck all gringos!"

I looked at him trying to decide what I ought
to do. It had me in kind of a tight fix. The last
thing I wanted in Sabinas was any trouble,
especially gun trouble, because they'd figure
out right quick that I was a little too familiar
with the *pistola* to be an honest rancher. And if
I got in trouble with a Mexican I'd be wrong,
no matter what I did or what I didn't do. And
that would be a nice way to get in with Linda's
daddy, by having a saloon fight my first day in
town. The man had his right side to the bar,
and I couldn't see his pistol, see what kind
it was and how he had it set up, to make a
judgment as to just how experienced he was. I
didn't figure he knew much or he wouldn't be
talking loud in bars and insulting strangers.

"Get out, you fucking gringo," he said to me.
"You make the bad smell in here, and you go
or maybe I keel me one gringo."

Well, now that was getting a little serious.
It didn't matter to me if he was drunk or not.
You're just as dead if a drunk kills you. And
he had me at the disadvantage of not wanting
any trouble. I kept hoping one of the men at
the table knew him and would intervene, but
they just watched silently.

It was making me look bad. Mexicans hate a
coward, and so far I hadn't showed them nothing. So the hell of it was that I was damned if I
did and damned if I didn't. I said, "Take it easy,
hombre. I don't want no trouble."

He came sliding down the bar to me, kind of hunched over. He wasn't a young man, maybe ten years older than I was. He had stringy hair that was going bald in the middle. He stopped about three feet away. I'd gotten a look at his weapon. He was carrying an old Navy Colt's .44, and his rigging wasn't set up in any proper fashion. But that didn't mean nothing. He'd done got so close that he couldn't miss, drunk or not. And he had me at the disadvantage that I didn't want to kill him. Then he was drunk, which made him unpredictable. A drunk gets whiskey brave and does things he ordinarily wouldn't do. And they're hard to read because of that false courage the liquor gives them. Oh, a drunk carrying a pistol that you don't want to kill is a dangerous thing indeed.

Now he was tapping me on the chest with that forefinger of his. "Fucking gringo," he said again.

I looked over at the men at the table, still hoping one of them would intervene, but they just stared without a flicker of emotion. I said to them, "Is this man a friend of any of you? He's drunk, and I don't want no trouble."

Which came out weak even in my own ears.

Old Pancho with the thinning hair had straightened up and pushed himself away from the bar. I thought that here was a man that severely wanted to get hisself killed. If he kept pushing he wadn't going to leave me no selection, and it was going to end bad for both of us. I was about to make up my mind to leave. I said to the men at the table: "I'm a stranger here who's come to go into the ranching business in this locale. Because of my connection with a prominent family hereabouts I can't afford any trouble. This man is obviously drunk."

The man said, slurring pretty badly now, "Fucking *cowardly* gringo. Your *madre es una puta.*"

Well he was really pushing having just called my mother a whore. I said to him: "Look, get away or you're going to get hurt. What's the matter with you anyway?"

I was still leaning against the bar, my left hand lightly holding my glass. I had my right hip kind of cocked up to make my draw easier. One thing, I sure as hell wasn't going to let him kill me so I was watching him plenty close. It was quiet in the place except when the drunk was talking. He tapped me on the chest and I shoved his hand away. It made him back up a step. He stood there swaying slightly and staring at me. "Fucking gringo," he said, and I knew he was going to draw about an instant before he did. My left hand was already sweeping my drink up as his right hand went down for his pistol. I threw the drink in his face just as he started out of the holster with that big Navy Colt's. I let him clear leather then slapped it out of his hand. It clattered to the floor, and I buried my left fist in his big soft belly. He went "Ooooff!" and bent over. I took a driving step forward and hit him a short chopping right on the side of the head. My fist hit his head, his head hit the edge of the bar, and he went down on his back in a sprawling heap.

Wasn't a sound in the saloon except the bartender had quit mopping up the bar. I reached down, got the drunk's pistol, emptied the cartridges out of it, and dropped it on his belly. Boy, it seemed like I just couldn't stay out of trouble, seemed like there was just something about me that made people want to go to war with me. But I felt like I'd gotten out of this mess about as well as I could. I looked over at the men at the table who were still staring, poker faced. "Who is this man?" I asked.

"Com'on," I said, "don't any of ya'll recognize this *hombre?* Is he a stranger?"

A distinguished gray-haired man cleared his throat. "He is a gentleman named Perales. He is a member of the *alcalde* council."

Oh, shit, I thought. He was on the mayor's council. In town one day and I'd slugged a member of the mayor's council. That such foul luck should have befallen me absolutely filled me with rage. I said, "I'll be go to hell!" Then I looked at them. "But if you knew this man why didn't you stop him? It was obvious he was drunk."

The gray-haired man shrugged. "Who can say?"

The man across from him said, "He is much trouble, that one, when he is drunk. It was not our affair."

"Well, look here," I said, "what the hell's the matter with him? How come he hates gringos?"

The gray-haired man laughed. "He has no especial feelings for gringos. You were here, you were a gringo. He was drunk. He always wants to fight when he is drunk. One excuse is as good as another."

"But do not bother yourself," one of them said. "He will be sober when he wakes up and will be no trouble. We have seen him thus many times. Still, he is a powerful man in the town, and it is to the best not to raise his ire."

I looked down at the drunk. He was breathing easily. He looked more like he was asleep than knocked out. Only a cut on the side of his head where I'd hit him and some early swelling gave it away that he'd been hurt. I said: "Well, hadn't we ought to try and get him home? I can't leave him laying here."

"It is quite all right," the gray-haired man said. "He lives at the hotel. The bartender will tell them at the desk, and they will take him to his room." He coughed. "It is unfortunate for you, señor, and a sorrow that you should have such an introduction to our city. But you must understand that he is a very good man when he is sober. He works very well at his job most of the day and has a very powerful following among the politicans and voters."

"How often does he get drunk?"

"Every afternoon."

"And he always wants to fight?"

"If there is a target, such as yourself, ready at hand."

I looked down at him and shook my head. "He's going to get hisself kilt."

"Perhaps so."

I made my adióses and went on up to my room, more than a little disturbed by the incident. For the next hour I sat on my bed and smoked *cigarrillos* and drank out of a bottle of whiskey I had on the nightstand. After a while there came a knock at my door and a boy brought me a note from Señor de Cava. It was in an envelope of good quality heavy paper with a crest up in the corner. I turned it over in my hands a few times before I opened it. I was more than a little nervous. Finally I got the note out and read it. It said that, of course, he, the don, remembered me, and that they would be delighted if I would call the next afternoon, and that I should be prepared to take the evening meal with them.

Well, boy, that tickled the hell out of me and relieved my mind just somewhat. I read the note again, and it didn't change. I tell you, you can't beat them quality folks for class. Even invited me to supper.

I had another drink to celebrate and then went on downstairs to get something to eat. I already knew the hotel had the best dining room in town, so I went in there. It was about half-full, and I'd already sat down at a table when I saw the drunk from the bar sitting over at a table in the corner eating steak. He didn't appear to be drunk anymore, but he looked pale and, even from the distance I was sitting, I could see the lump up side of his head where I'd hit him.

I looked at him a moment wondering if I ought to do something. I damn sure wasn't going to apologize, but I thought it might make matters better for the future if I went over and asked if he was all right. Finally, I just decided to hell with it. Maybe I'd tell Don de Cava of the incident and ask his advice. Or maybe nothing would ever come of it.

The man never looked up. I ordered my supper and was eating it when he walked right by me with no sign of recognition. It made me feel a little relieved. Maybe he was one of those kind of drunks who never remember what they've done or what happened when they sober up. If such was the case I was worrying myself for nothing.

After supper I strolled out on the town with a good feeling in me. I stood on the side of the street wondering if they had a whorehouse in the town. That week with Cata had got my juices flowing again, and I'd got used to not being without it. And it had been a spell, even though I'd been sick and hurt part of the time. Finally I decided not. There was plenty of time for everything. What I'd do this night was have me a good stroll around town in the cool of the night then get a good rest in a real bed for a change. I tell you, I was beginning to look on the next morning as the start of some kind of new life.

CHAPTER 10

The next day passed about as slow as a day can pass. I had breakfast, then didn't do much of anything except sit around smoking until lunchtime. After lunch I walked down to a saloon and got in a small stakes poker game, but I couldn't concentrate. The place was quiet and dead except for the game, which was about half-Mexicans and about half–Texas cowboys. I had a few drinks, though I planned to hold it down on the whiskey, then sweated the time out to about three-thirty and went on back to the hotel. I'd kept asking the bartender what time it was so often that one of the cowboys finally asked me if I was taking medicine.

Back at the hotel I had me another bath and then went down to a barbershop and had my hair cut and got me a store-bought shave. Oh, I was getting dandified all right. I'd figured thirty minutes for a ride out to Señor de Cava's rancho, and I wanted to be there by five, so I went to the hotel and dressed in my soft breeches and frilly shirt and went on over to the livery stable and saddled up and headed it out the road I'd been over the one time before.

Well, I went along feeling like I'd done the best I could to make myself presentable. I'd left orders at the livery stable to have my horse brushed down and my saddle and rigging cleaned and oiled and rubbed. I'd even had my boots blacked. I tell you, the money I'd laid out for this one meeting would have kept a family in groceries for a month. I'd spent nearly forty dollars on clothes, twenty dollars of it being for the very shirt and britches I was wearing. Then that hair cut and shave and the two baths was another three dollars. But of course I didn't care. I had plenty of money. But my thinking about it just shows you how broke I'd been that two years. Hell, if I'd had forty dollars at one time then I'd a thought I was rich.

Don Fernando de Cava's place was about four miles out of town. You first went south on the Monterrey road for about three miles, then turned off to the right over a little wagon track that wound its way back through the cactus and chaparral and mesquite and the baking land that scarce looked like it'd support one cow, much less the considerable herds of cattle and horses that Señor de Cava was supposed to run.

The country was pretty flat, though here and there it rose up into a little hill or dropped off in a sheer gully. I rode easy and slow, trying to keep from sweating up my new clothes in the mid-afternoon heat. I might should have come later. Them high-class Mexicans don't sometime take supper until as late as eight o'clock. But I'd been running on Texas time, and I was mighty anxious in the bargain. Well, going early would give Don Fernando another chance to show off his horse herd to me and maybe we could even talk some business about me buying horses from him. Or at least brood mares, because I planned to use Texas horses for stud to breed for size. As a general rule Mexican horses were too small for my tastes.

I had mentally figured up what it was going to cost me to get in the horse business. I figured two thousand dollars would make a very handsome down payment on the land. I wasn't going to raise range horses, and therefore I wouldn't need over five or six thousand acres for the kind of operation I had in mind. And with this type of land selling for fifty cents to a dollar an acre, I'd be able to get cranked up pretty easy. Then I figured on about sixty brood mares and about six or seven good stallions. I reckoned that would take another four to five thousand, leaving me somewhere around seven thousand to get some kind of house built and to live on until the horse herd started producing.

Of course I wasn't going to fool with cattle. I didn't know a damn thing about raising cattle and had no taste for it. But horses was a subject I damn well knew. As did most people in the line of work I'd followed.

I just rode along like that, thinking about the future, and pretty soon I'd raised the Rancho Fernando. I swept in under the porticoed gate and put the horse in a lope for the house.

It was about as grand as I'd remembered. It was white adobe with a red-tile roof and seemed bigger than a church. There was one main breezeway right through the center of the house, but there were others that opened along the sides. The grounds were neat and well kept and there was some twenty or thirty outbuildings, barns and sheds and houses for the ranch workers and their families. A piece to the west of the house were the corrals with a bunch of horses in them.

I rode up in front and hallooed the house, not dismounting. After a minute a peon came out, and I told him who I was and that Don Fernando was expecting me. He disappeared inside and then come flying back out in a minute or so, and I dismounted and let him take my horse and went on in, self-consciously dusting myself off with my hat.

I went down the main entrance hall and turned into what I guess you'd call the parlor. The last time I'd been there they'd greeted me formally. The don and his wife had been seated while their three girls and two boys had been standing by their side. They were just like that this time only two were missing. The oldest boy, who'd been sixteen at the time, wasn't there.

Neither was Linda.

My heart dropped as I went in the room, but I never let on, just went up to the don as he arose and shook hands.

"Mr. Wilson!" he said smiling.

"Don Fernando."

"It has been such a long time, my friend." Señor de Cava was a tall, slimly built man with a big mustache and glossy, slicked-back hair. He was wearing a good suit of linen clothes with a brocaded vest on underneath. One look at him and the way he handled himself and you knew he'd been raised to quality. I never thought much about manners until I run into some high-class *hombre* like Don Fernando and seen the way he made it look.

We finished greeting, and then I bowed to his wife and he took me down the line to say hello to his kids. The two girls were there, giggling as they had the two years back, and the youngest boy, now beginning to look like a man himself. We got all that done, and then Don Fernando directed me into a chair and had me brandy and a cigar brought. We got lit up, made a toast, and then settled back. Me and him and his wife was kind of arranged in a little semi-circle. The kids had come in apparently just to greet me for now they all asked to be excused. I watched them leaving.

"A man who has children like that," I said, "can count himself a success no matter what happens the rest of his life."

The don beamed. He was a stone family man. "You are most kind to say that, Señor Wilson.

But tell me, what have you been doing in the time since we saw you last? I had expected you to come back to visit us while you were here the last time. But I had occasion to inquire about you on an errand in town, and it was to my surprise that you had left."

"Yes," I said, "I was called away unexpectedly." I said it wondering what he'd think if I'd told him what I'd been called away unexpectedly for. To kill the two men who'd murdered Les. But I went ahead and answered his first question. I'd made me up a cock-and-bull story to cover the past two years. Something about horse trading and losing a ranch because of lack of rain. Just something I figured he'd believe. I told it mechanically, not thinking about it, while I wondered where Linda was and wondered how I could inquire after her without showing my real interest.

When I finished the don said sympathetically, "Ah, yes, that is very bad luck, the lack of rain. But that is a gamble one takes in the ranching business, no?"

I agreed with him then casually noted that his oldest boy hadn't been in the line up when I'd come in. "I hope he's all right."

"Ah, yes," Don Fernando said. "I am very proud of him. He is presently attending the university in Mexico City and shows promise of becoming a scholar, something I would never have expected from him." He laughed heartily at what he thought was a good joke.

My mood, however, was not so light. I hadn't
given a damn where his son was, I was only
using it in hopes he'd mention Linda. "Well,
that is something to be proud of," I said. "Yes,
indeed." I drew on my cigar and tried to think
of some other way to ask.

But the don was saying, "Ah, Señor Wilson,
too bad that you could not have been here six
months ago. My daughter Linda— You recall
my daughter Linda, my eldest?"

If the don could have known just how often
I'd recalled his daughter Linda and just what
I'd done to get back here and have a run at her
hand he'd of been more than a little provoked.
But I just said, "Yes."

"Of course. You had previously met her at
my brother's, is that not so?"

I looked at the end of my cigar. I kept my
voice steady. "Yes."

"Six months ago we had a wonderful wedding here. She was married. Ah, what a *fies-
ta*!"

"It was wonderful!" his wife said.

But she could have been saying the cat was
on fire for all I was hearing her. I felt the
way I had when the man had hit me in the
belly with an ax handle when we were robbing
the mercantile store in Freer. I couldn't speak,
couldn't do anything. The best I could do was
reach for my brandy glass and take it all down
in one, gulping swallow.

The don said: "She married a wonderful
young man. A physician from Monterrey. Ah

yes, a very fine young man. Perhaps you will have the chance to meet him someday, Señor Wilson. I'm sure you would be friends. You both seem of the same age."

But I couldn't hear him either. All I knew was the sick, empty feeling inside me and the need to get away, to be off by myself. I didn't want to stay here in the house where there was no Linda. I didn't want to eat supper with the don and his wife and other kids. I didn't want to sit here and listen to their prattle. I wanted to be gone. I felt like there was a band around my chest cutting off my air. I had to leave. But I couldn't let on what a blow I'd just taken. I wasn't about to let them know.

"Well, that's certainly fine," I finally mumbled. "Hope she'll be very happy." Even though it was cool in the room I could feel myself beginning to sweat. The don was looking at me intently.

"Are you all right, Señor Wilson?" he asked.

"No," I said, "I am not well. I was taken ill on the ride out from town but I elected to come ahead and visit a few moments before going back to town. I was wounded a few weeks ago in a raid on my cattle ranch, and I have not been well since."

"You should have said!" he proclaimed. He jumped to his feet. "I will have a room prepared for you immediately."

"No," I said. "No, no, no. I must go back to town."

"I won't hear of it."

"No, I have to see the doctor." I was really sweating now. I stood up, and I actually felt dizzy on my feet.

"I'll send for him."

"No, no, no," I said. "It's all arranged. I must return. I'll come again in a few days when I'm better. If you'll just have my horse brought up."

He continued to protest while I thought I was going to faint if I didn't get away. In the end he sent for my horse and then insisted on seeing me off. I made the best adiós I could to his wife then went down the hall and outside.

It was one of the hardest chores I've ever had to stand there, waiting for my horse, and try to be civil and make conversation with Don Fernando. He kept chattering away, but I was so numb I barely heard a word he was saying. When my horse finally came I swung gratefully into the saddle. Don Fernando wanted to send someone to ride with me to be sure I reached town all right.

"No, no," I said. "I will be all right." I touched my hat and wheeled my horse before he could say another word and rode out of there.

I rode fast for the first mile, running my horse. After a time I pulled him down to a gallop and then a trot and then a walk and then I stopped him and dismounted. I had been carefully keeping my mind a blank. But now I stood close to my horse and put my chin on the seat of the saddle and stared out across the prairie. I didn't know what to think, didn't know what to do. If I had known how to cry I believe I would have wept at that very moment. I had longed for what I had hoped to build and to have for so long that to have it suddenly taken away was the bitterest blow I've ever been dealt. And to have the someone, Linda, who was to have been instrumental in my plan suddenly placed beyond my reach was almost more than I could bear. I felt very alone, very lonely, and very sure that what I sought was never going to be mine no matter what I did.

I stood like that a long time, staring out at the prairie. Well, I guess I'd had no right to expect it anyway. What was I but a common outlaw with no more business aspiring to marry the daughter of quality than a pig wishing for roller skates. Hell, I'd wanted to be respectable. Did I think buying a horse ranch was going to make me respectable? Buying it with money I'd stolen off a train? Hell, who was I kidding. I was Wilson Young, the outlaw, and I was never going to be anything else.

I thought about it, seeing a life of succeeding years like the years I'd already lived. A life of being on the run, a life of having every man's hand against me.

I breathed hard. I didn't think I could stand more years of the same. I was getting too old for such a life, a life I hadn't particularly wanted in the first place. I knew I was slowing down, knew my will was weakening. It wouldn't be long before I come off second in one of them gunfights, and that would be the finish of me.

I don't know how long I stood there. It was long enough so that my mood gradually began to change. I finally kind of come to and swung up in the saddle. No, I would not give up. I had me a plan, and I had me the money to carry it out. All I'd lost was the woman, and all that meant was I wasn't going to be able to borrow respectability from her. Well, that would just have to be. But I wasn't going to give up.

I started riding, and I began to evolve another plan. I'd go back to Sabinas and wire Cata at her brother's in San Antonio to get on the train and come to Nuevo Laredo. Then I'd go and get her and bring her back, and we'd go in the ranching business in the little green valley. No one would know Cata in Sabinas Hidalgo, and she'd be just as respectable as anybody.

It give me a pang when I thought about what I was losing and what I was taking in her place. But no matter. Cata was a good woman, and she'd work hard to make me happy. I knew she would. Maybe I was better off. Maybe I wouldn't have liked the daughter of a don who'd been used to riches and luxury all her life. She was probably spoiled. But Cata would appreciate everything I did for her. She would appreciate what I was trying to do and would go through the hardships and sacrifices without a whimper.

I began to ride faster. It was still good daylight for at that time of year the days were very long. My mind was still reeling, but I was thinking hard as I rode. I didn't know that I could stand to stay in Sabinas for the first little while. Perhaps I would wire Cata and then start immediately for Nuevo Laredo. Perhaps I would leave this very night. I felt restless and nervous and very unsure of just what I wanted to do.

But one thing I knew; I had to try and make me a place somewhere with whatever woman I could find. I could not go back to the life I had been living.

Before I knew it I was entering the town. I rode to the hotel and dismounted and tied my horse and went inside even though I still wasn't sure what I ought to do. For a moment I stood in the lobby, trying to think. It ain't often that I get a blow that just slam knocks the sense out of my head, but that's the way I felt standing there. Finally I decided to hell with it. I was too restless to sit and wait for Cata. I'd wire her and then go down to Nuevo Laredo and wait for her there. It'd give me something to be doing. So what I'd do would be to go down to the livery stable, pay my bill, come on back to the hotel and pack what little stuff I had, pay my bill, and go and wire Cata. Then leave town.

I turned around and went back outside and started for the livery stable, which was just around the corner. There were considerable number of people on the street, it being Saturday. A couple of times I had to take my horse around a little clump that stood there talking in the dusty street.

I got to the livery stable and dismounted and tied my horse up out front. I was just about to go in the door when I heard a shot. I figured it was some *campesino* celebrating being in town, and I kind of glanced casually toward the corner where the hotel was.

The drunk, the mayor's councilman, was running straight toward me firing his pistol.

It shocked me at first, and then a kind of cold rage took me. It was one too many. I was tired of being fucked with. I had done a good enough job messing up my life, and I didn't need no help from anyone.

I watched the fool coming on, stepping well clear of my horse as I did. He fired again, the bullet going wild. Anybody with any sense knows you don't run and fire a handgun at the same time. It makes your eyes jounce up and down as well as your gun hand, and you ain't got a Chinaman's chance of hitting anything.

Well, this son of a bitch had fucked around with me all I was going to stand for. I let him get about twenty yards away, and then I pulled my revolver, went down on one knee, and shot him square in the chest.

It was as if he had run into a wall. One second he was running and the next it was like he'd come to a dead stop. Then he slowly went over on his back.

I walked toward him, holding my gun down by my side. I was dimly conscious that the hubbub from the square had stilled and that it was very quiet. I got to the mayor's councilman and looked down at him. He was killed all right.

I went back and got my horse and walked, leading him to the hotel. There was a crowd drawn across the street, watching silently. They fell back and made a lane as I approached. I still had my pistol in my hand, holding it down by my side.

As I walked I was thinking. I was thinking that I was never going to get things put to rights. I'd lost the girl and swallowed that, and now a drunk that I didn't even know had caused the rest of my plans to go a-glimmering. It had been self-defense, all right, but I was a gringo in Mexico, and the dead drunk had been a mayor's councilman. Even if I didn't get hung or put in jail it would be a long period of trouble, and I wasn't in the mood for that. I didn't want no part of being in the law's hands, Mexican or U.S. I kept walking steadily for the hotel. I wasn't going to run. If law came before I left, they'd have to deal with me with a revolver in my hand and rage in my heart.

I got to the hotel and tied my horse. Before I went in I swept my eyes around the crowd that had dogged my footsteps. They fell back ever so little.

I went into the hotel. My mind was strangely calm. I was angry, but I was also resigned. It was not a good mood for anyone to fool with me unless he wanted an early end to his life.

Part of the crowd followed me into the lobby, but I paid them no mind, just went on upstairs and packed my gear into my saddlebags, slung them over my shoulder, and went back down.

At the desk I asked the clerk for my bill. He stared at me, his eyes big and round in his face. "Give me my bill, goddamnit!" I said. It took him another second to recover, but then he did though he was still so nervous he could barely write out the receipt. I paid and went out through the door and tied my saddlebags on the back of my horse. There was still no sign of any law.

And then I was ready, ready to leave the place I'd spent two years and several lives trying to get to. A wedding and a drunken councilman were the cause of my leaving.

Finally I mounted and turned my horse out into the street. A man in a uniform came running toward me calling out, "Señor, señor! You wait!"

I pointed my pistol at him. "Go to hell," I said. He almost fell down trying to scramble away. I looked around at the faces staring up at me and then touched my horse with my spurs, lifting him into a high lope.

I rode north up the main street until the edge of town. There I stopped and looked back at the place I'd meant to call my home. I no longer had any plans or even very much hope. The gold was still in the bank. I'd get it someday. Until then it was in as good a place as any. It hadn't bought me any of the things I'd expected it would.

I took one last look then turned resolutely toward the north and spurred my horse into a run. It always seemed as if I were leaving something rather than going to someplace. It was not a good feeling.